BESO DULCE

RAYANNE SINCLAIR

Hopetoun Publishing
Edmonds, Washington

BESO DULCE
Rayanne Sinclair
Copyright © 2014 by Rayanne Sinclair

HOPETOUN PUBLISHING
Edmonds, Washington

For more information about this book, visit
www.rayannesinclair.com

Print ISBN 978-0-9897502-2-6
Electronic ISBN 978-0-9897502-3-3

This is dedicated to the ones I like

Acknowledgements

This book was developed in conjunction with the same wonderful team of professionals as my first book, *Steal Away*. Therefore, I want to acknowledge Nancy Wick, Beth Jusino, Jenn Reese, and Kathy Burge for their patience and goodness to me. Special thanks also to Laura, my friend and traveling companion for research on this book. I hope this team will continue working together until there are no more stories in me.

Lastly, I want to thank Barbara Perkins, who was such a wonderful guide and hostess in the lovely town of Todos Santos.

CHAPTER 1

Crossing the stage in the line with fellow University of Southern California graduates, she heard the dean read her name, "Katarina Steiner, Bachelor of Arts, Art History, magna cum laude." After shaking the dean's hand, Kat walked off the platform and held her diploma up to the sky. She hoped that her parents might be looking down to watch this event. After all, it was in their honor that she was even walking the aisle on this sunny June afternoon in the centennial year of the university.

As she dutifully listened to the speeches of the newly appointed university president and the female guest speaker, she couldn't help but think it was a cruel hoax that her graduation date fell on the one-year anniversary of the death of her parents in a horrendous automobile accident on a California freeway. This June 7 was just a reminder of her loss on June 7, 1979, when at the age of 20, Kat had been left alone in this world, without siblings or any other relatives in this country. And how she longed for her parents to share in this major life event, but she'd have to settle for her best friend, Barb Beasley.

As Kat rounded the corner to return to her seat under the banner of the School of Fine Arts, she could see Barb in the following section of graduates from the School of Education. Barb was waving frantically, missing out on the cues for her row to stand up and start making their way to the waiting line. That's Barb, thought Kat, forgetting everything else, but never her friends.

Holding it together through the entire commencement, Kat took some joy in knowing that at least she didn't yet have to be alone this evening. Once the mortar boards flew into the air and the band played "Pomp and Circumstance," she'd catch up with Barb's family to stay at their home just 30 minutes away in Pasadena.

After the ceremony, the graduates located each other in the crowd and took off for Kat's new white convertible Mercedes. They'd soon be heading up the highway with the convertible top down and the radio blasting. With the wind whipping through Barb's shoulder-length strawberry blonde hair, the two were singing along with their favorite Blondie tunes. The last four years had been loads of fun, and yet they were both feeling a great relief from their con- centrated efforts and were now ready to let it rip.

While Barb was born and raised in southern California, Kat was a California girl only by virtue of vacationing there over the years. Though her permanent address would now be her family's summer home in Carmel, she had matric- ulated at USC as an out-of-state student from Evanston, Illinois. That was because her father's business was head- quartered on the Loop in Chicago. However, Johannes and Liesl Steiner had retired to the beach cottage in Carmel when Kat started her sophomore year at USC, making her a California resident now. So tomorrow she'd drive "home" with all her college belongings stuffed into the small trunk of the car she'd recently bought for herself using some of the life insurance monies.

The after party at the Beasleys' was great fun, in large measure because Barb's family was the only complete family Kat felt she had. Standing up at the head of the table after dinner, Mr. Beasley proposed a toast with, "To accomplishment and friendship, may you lovely ladies continue in both."

With that, Barb's comedic older brother added, "Hear, hear...to accomplishship and friendment!" In addition to making her laugh, Steve Beasley was a perpetual charmer of Kat, though he knew it was strictly platonic based on her repeatedly declaring him her "only brother." Barb and Kat had that discussion about two years ago, the one in which Barb whispered over their textbooks in the library that she gave Kat her permission to date her brother. Only one problem, there was no chemistry 101 there. Nonetheless, Kat enjoyed Steve to no end, and tonight she was soaking up the attention for tomorrow she knew she'd be alone.

CHAPTER 2

The friends said their tearful goodbyes in the driveway the next morning after breakfast. It wasn't as though they'd never see each other again, but neither one was sure where life would take them now.

"Barb, keep in mind that you have a standing invitation to come visit me anytime in Carmel," said Kat as she leaned over to hug her freckle-faced, five-foot-three-inch best friend.

"You know I will make the drive north when I get some time off from my new job, Kat," replied Barb.

Having received an offer of a teaching job in a school for the deaf, Barb was eager to get started; she also wanted Kat to know their friendship was a promise. To make the message even clearer, Barb crossed her arms over the front of her chest and then pointed to Kat. Given that Barb had taught Kat some sign language, Kat knew she was sending love her way.

Kat and Barb had met just four years earlier at a freshman orientation event that involved food, music, and information tables about various clubs and activities on campus. The two immediately hit it off as they ended up seated next to each other and realized they were assigned to the same dorm. As their freshman year proceeded, they continued to build their friendship by studying together, meeting up in the dining hall, and attending some concerts and sporting events together. So it was only natural that they ended up being roommates for all three of their subsequent years on campus. And, of course, it was Barb and her family members who had cared for Kat during the darkest days after losing her parents.

Starting up the car this morning, Kat had determined she'd make this an all-day affair by taking the scenic coastal route up Highway 101. With the warm wind in her long, thick, beige-blonde hair, she was feeling such a mix of emotions today. There were moments when she felt strong, capable, and content, and yet 30 minutes down the road, she'd experience feelings of uncertainty, loneliness, and anxiety. She was intelligent enough to know that the mind works overtime on the emotions, but her usual rational self-talk just didn't seem to come easily on this drive.

After stopping for a light lunch and a bit of shopping in Santa Barbara, Kat decided to take a walk on the beach. Taking off her sandals and tossing them into her purse, she thought of this as her chapel service this Sunday morning. She blocked out the people and spent her time concentrating on her God and His Word, asking Him to order her steps in the way He would have her go in life. Remembering her parents, Kat acknowledged that anything could happen to cut a life short, yet in her prime, it seemed like the life ahead of her was as expansive as the coastline she was walking.

It certainly wasn't as if Kat would likely ever want for anything in this life. Johannes Steiner had spent a lifetime in the international diamond and precious metals business. Her father had been a brilliant businessman who had established a trust with all the family assets totaling millions, which were hers upon turning 21 earlier in the year. At this point, Kat's fortune was in the capable hands of Larry Barnes, an incredible friend, confidant, and financial advisor to the family for nearly 20 years.

Kat trusted Larry a great deal with her property, and also for general advice in life. It was Larry, after all, who had prayed for her parents for so long. His godly life example, witness, and prayers led her parents to the Lord when she was just a toddler. Kat was so grateful to have been raised in a loving Christian home with parents who were transformational people in their own right. Now 64 years old, Larry was one of the few trusted advisors Kat had left. Her thoughts drifted to his gracious and insightful words at the memorial service for her parents and how present Larry and his wife had been for her afterward.

Kat's memories reached back further as she recalled hearing the story when she was old enough to understand, the one about how her parents had met Larry back in Chicago after being referred to him by a business associate. Larry, who was also an attorney, had a good reputation in the Windy City, both as a money manager and as an estate planner. The business relationship turned personal when Larry invited the Steiner family over to his home in the suburbs for dinner and later invited them to attend church with his family one Sunday. Growing up, Kat never really knew a time when her parents weren't believers, but apparently it was at a home Bible study in the Barnes living room where Larry led Liesl and Johannes in prayer as they committed their lives to the Lord.

Larry had made the first step to retirement when he moved to Monterey a few years ago. He claimed he wanted to improve his golf game, but nobody was convinced he was getting much more time on the links given how quickly

California clients had found him. Now back on the road, Kat made a mental note to set up lunch soon with Larry near his office in Monterey, just a few miles from her cottage.

Kat pulled into her driveway off Scenic Road in Carmel around dinnertime. The lovely two-bedroom place held such fond memories for her, and yet she'd not really lived in it for any stretch of time. Her vacations and school breaks had brought her here for periods of weeks, but now she'd be settling down in this pretty residential town. She wondered out loud to herself as she parked the car in the small garage, "Now what?"

After hauling her belongings into the house from her trunk, she dropped them in the master bedroom that she would now occupy. It seemed strange to be taking up residence in her parents' old bedroom rather than the bedroom upstairs that still held a mess of her stuffed animals. She made another mental note to herself about redecorating the home to make it her own. She hadn't touched things for the year her parents had been gone, but she was now ready to do so.

CHAPTER 3

Finding only stale saltines and a can of soda pop in the kitchen for dinner the night before, Kat woke up with a powerful hunger the next morning. However, she had gotten a good night's sleep in the downy soft queen-size bed. Now making her way to the private bath off the master suite, she took a long look at her sleepy self in the mirror and wondered how quickly she could dress and get to the local grocer to stock the fridge and cupboards. She figured she could be pretty quick, given how much her stomach was growling.

After washing up and throwing on a pair of jeans and a boatneck shirt that she found in her half-unpacked suitcase, she was ready to head into the quaint beach town for food. On her way out the door, she once again stopped by the full-length mirror in the bedroom, only to see her leggy five-foot-eight-inch form staring back at her, looking pretty unkempt. Pushing past what she saw, she headed out to the one-car garage.

Carmel was its usual gorgeous self that morning with some low-hanging clouds that would typically burn off to a beautiful sunny day. Having left the television on at the house, on her way out the door, she'd heard the meteorologist say that it should hit 78 degrees that day. The radio news in the car confirmed the same thing. The realization set in for Kat that she was relying on audio voices as a crutch right now as she transitioned from a people-filled life to one of solitude.

Arriving at the small local grocery store, Kat filled her cart with items that looked good to her while admitting to herself that she might want to get better organized about running her household. As she finished placing the grocery bags in the trunk of her car, she pulled out the carton of milk and a small package of powdered donuts she had purchased to eat along the way. Driving home she stuffed her face with the donuts and ground the traces of the fallen white powdered sugar into her jeans. With hunger now at bay, Kat was reenergized for the chores ahead of her. She had her list that included doing laundry, putting away all her stuff and storing the suitcases, and making that call to Larry.

By noon Kat had made enough progress that she stopped to make a sandwich and sit out on the patio to enjoy her ocean view and the red bougainvillea that draped over the lattice work there. Still needing to hear another human voice, she had turned up the radio in the nearby kitchen so she could hear it outside through the screen door.

"*Our program today brings the visual arts to our radio listeners. How is that possible, you ask?*" inquired the host of his invisible audience. This should be interesting, Kat thought to herself, art on an audio-only medium! As an art history major with a minor in sculpture, she was already hooked.

The radio host spent the hour talking with a curator from the Louvre in Paris. They focused on Canova's marble work of *Psyche Revived by Cupid's Kiss*. The curator discussed its history, the story of the goddess, and what the artist went through to develop the complex piece. Kat had only seen pictures of the work and thought it was stunningly sensual, as near to perfection as any human artist could derive. The radio discussion began to fade into the background, replaced by her dreams of going to Paris with enough time to wander for days through the Louvre.

Finally breaking free of her daydream, she picked up the phone to call Larry Barnes. "Hi, Larry, it's Kat! How are you doing?"

Larry responded with a cheery, "I'm doing well but so busy these days that you've caught me eating lunch at my desk."

"Having lunch here too," echoed Kat. "If you'd like, I could pass the chips and dip through the phone to you!"

Larry chuckled as he reflected upon how much Kat shared her mother's sense of humor. The two had a great catch-up session as Larry congratulated her on the diploma and her academic honors. Kat asked to set a date for lunch later in the week to get him out of the office. They decided on Friday at noon when she'd meet him in Monterey at one of the family's favorite restaurants.

CHAPTER 4

Kat drove into Monterey a bit early in order to find parking and walk the wharf for a time before meeting up with Larry at Old Fisherman's Grotto. Passing some sleepy brown pelicans perched in the sun, she decided to find a nearby bench where she could observe them as well as the people. She loved living near the water and couldn't imagine ever returning to the Midwest where she had spent her formative years. She was taking in the salty air and feeling the warmth of the sun on her face when Larry arrived. As the two hugged before heading into the restaurant for lunch, Kat couldn't help but notice that the tall but stocky man, who had sported a head of thick jet black hair when she was growing up, now had a receding hairline, and what hair remained was something closer to salt and pepper in color.

Now seated at their table, Kat opened with, "So, Larry, if there's any business I need to take care of, can we get that out of the way first?"

"Sure thing, Kat," Larry assured her.

No sooner had they placed their order than Larry pulled a few documents out of his leather binder. Pushing them over to Kat, he explained, "These are release forms for you to sign allowing me to complete the sale of shares in an Australian diamond mine. The mine was one of the first your father bought into over two decades ago. However, due to recent labor unrest, I believe it's time to release the asset."

Hearing about her father's purchase made so long ago almost made it seem sentimental, except that Kat knew it wasn't something her father would want her to feel that way about. When she asked Larry what this transaction would mean for her assets, he went into a lengthy diatribe about reinvestment, tax avoidance, and rebalancing her portfolio. All this was enough to cause her to change the subject as soon as their food arrived.

"Larry, I think I would like to do some work on the cottage and take a trip to Europe. Of course, not in that order. I'd start the work on the cottage after returning from Europe."

Larry looked puzzled and responded with, "Any particular part of Europe, Kat?" She remembered that her father had always told her that he never kept secrets from Larry, so she began to pour out her heart to him.

"Well, while I'd like to go to Paris to tour the art museums for a few days, I'm definitely feeling the need to see some family, Larry. The only blood relatives I have are those my parents left back in the old country."

Larry reached over and patted her hand in understanding. "Kat, Paris sounds great, and I think it may be a necessity for you to bring some closure to your losses. It may also end up having the same benefit for your relatives in Austria. I'll transfer some funds from your trust to both your checking and savings accounts to cover the trip and the upgrades on the cottage when you return."

As they ate lunch, Larry had Kat talking about her graduation and how she was settling into the cottage in Carmel.
Larry was such a kind man who always took an interest in
others. Before they parted that afternoon, Larry prayed for
Kat right there in the booth, asking the Lord to give her safe
travels and favor wherever she placed her feet. No sooner
did he finish with a strong "Amen!" than Kat chimed in with,
"Thanks for everything, Larry. I'll send you a postcard when
I get to Vienna!"

On her way out of town, Kat stopped at a local travel
agency. Working with a woman named Judy, she made
plans to depart on June 22 for Vienna via Paris. Though she
had an open invite from her paternal grandparents, Margrit
and Arne Steiner, Kat felt she should stay in a hotel for the
several days she'd be there. That would allow her to visit
with them, as well as her father's sister, her unmarried Aunt
Annika Steiner, and perhaps even other relatives she'd never
met. But first she would travel to Paris to spend several
days. She was determined to take in the entire Louvre and
as much of the city's art as she could before returning home.
Judy had Kat's itinerary written down and promised to be in
touch with confirmation numbers and tickets by next week.

CHAPTER 5

Over the next several days, Kat waded through the process of separating things that she wanted to donate from things she wanted to keep in the cottage. She'd done plenty of cleaning too, and even rearranged the furniture a bit more to her liking. To relax, she'd found time to do some paper art depicting pretty white shells in relief. She was happy with how the project turned out and figured she'd frame the work in a shadow box to hang it in the beach house.

By mid-week, the mailman had brought by a few bills and the large envelope from Judy at the travel agency. Within days, Kat would be packing and then heading up to the San Francisco airport to fly out to Paris with a plane change in New York. She thought about how light she'd be able to travel due to the warmer weather, and she wanted to leave plenty of room for things she'd purchase there. As she pondered that idea, her mind wandered to how fun it might be to find a beautiful haute couture dress in Paris. Not altogether sure that she'd have any place to wear it in casual California, she dismissed the whole idea as extravagant. However, she could feel herself getting excited about the travel and the sights, despite the fact that she'd be doing it alone.

17

On the morning of Sunday, June 22, Kat had her suitcase in the car and was locking up the cottage for her European vacation. The first part of this trip meant a two-hour drive to the San Francisco airport, so she made sure to have plenty of coffee in her travel thermos. Arriving around 11:00 a.m. for her 1:00 p.m. flight, she left her car in long-term parking and took a shuttle that dropped her off at her airline ticketing location. Checking her bag through, she was finally left with just her oversized handbag into which she had dropped a book that she found at the small memorial library in Carmel. It was an old book on art history that the library had thrown on the discard pile for patrons to take at will and keep. While it was outdated, Kat was still interested in perusing the contents. Settling in at her gate, she pulled it out and started reading and looking at the photos.

It seemed like she didn't get but a few pages into the book when the first call was made for boarding. She wasn't exactly eager to be stuffed into the plane as this day was going to be very long, into the next day, in fact. Making a trip to the ladies room and waiting until the last possible minute, she finally had to board and to get situated in her aisle seat about midway into the coach section.

Kat had thought about flying first class, which she certainly could have afforded, but the voice of her mother always came back to her about such things. Liesl Steiner had known hard times growing up in Vienna, and she never wanted Kat to take their prosperity for granted. Besides, her parents simply weren't people who flaunted their wealth. Kat grew up knowing she was better off than some but never really having a sense of how much better until Larry had briefed her on their estate upon the death of her parents. Despite that, she would continue their tradition of moderation. Similarly, she hoped to continue their tradition of charity. That, too, was a discussion she thought she'd need to have with Larry upon her return.

Fatigued from the first flight, Kat ducked into a ladies room in the New York airport to freshen up before making the connecting flight to Paris. Coming out of the stall to wash her hands, she stared at the mirror to assess the damage. Brushing her long hair, she twisted it around a wooden chopstick-like hair bob that held it in place upon her head. At least it was up off her neck as she was feeling warmer in this airport, despite the airport's claims of being temperature controlled. Adding a bit of lip gloss, she felt a bit more presentable.

All the fuss in the bathroom didn't go unnoticed as Kat captured a double take from one young man as she walked toward her connecting gate. Kat didn't think of herself as all that attractive and rarely spent much time or effort on her appearance. However, what most women needed to enhance was, in fact, natural beauty for Kat. She was tall and perfectly proportioned at 120 pounds and really didn't need makeup due to her gorgeous complexion, symmetrical facial features, beautiful steel blue eyes, and a smile that would send any young man to the moon and back. That was, when she did smile. Lately, those were becoming few and far between, and even she was conscious of it.

The layover in New York had been a long one, so Kat had had plenty of time to pick up snacks and a magazine at a small shop before boarding. Once again, she settled into an aisle seat that Judy had seen to for all her flights. After all, those long legs needed some place to stretch out. Besides, one of Kat's pet peeves was crawling over people to get to the restroom or walk the aisle on these longer flights. Having requested a blanket and pillow for this overnight flight, she was ready to go. And the older woman seated at the window next to her was already buried in her Agatha Christie novel as the plane taxied onto the runway for takeoff.

CHAPTER 6

Arriving in the City of Light on the afternoon of the next day, Kat made her way through all the required checkpoints in the airport. Her passport would receive one more stamp among the many she had collected growing up. Her mind was now on getting a cab to the hotel as quickly as possible. She was eager to take a shower and get some real sleep in a real bed before venturing out into the city this evening.

The travel agent had booked Kat in a new hotel, which had only about a dozen rooms. It was very nicely appointed in typical French furnishings and had a library and patio. The place was strategically selected by Judy because it was so close to the gardens, museums, restaurants, and shopping. Kat would need her walking shoes, but she was definitely up for that.

After a brief nap in her beautiful duvet-covered bed, Kat was ready to find dinner on the town. She didn't have to go far to find a lovely café with outdoor tables where she ordered what turned out to be an exquisite meal with a glass of French red wine. Feeling the warmth on her cheeks after finishing the wine, she was ready to study the map she had obtained from the concierge at the hotel. She needed to plan her route for tomorrow and the following days in order to get the most out of this trip.

After about an hour, Kat decided she'd taken up space at her table for so long that she'd better order dessert too. She figured that would give her the "right" to stay a bit longer to watch the people and enjoy the lovely summer evening in Paris. Not really knowing what she was ordering, she pointed to the La Côte Basque's Dacquoise which turned out to be an absolutely delightful mix of meringue, chocolate, nuts, and buttercream. Finishing the entire thing, Kat realized she'd need to go easy on the feasting here, lest she gain several pounds on this trip!

The next morning Kat was up early to bathe and put on a pretty sundress and comfortable flats that were tried and tested for walking. She hit the sidewalk—full of eager anticipation and quickly found a bakery where she could grab a croissant and coffee on her way to the Louvre. She hadn't intended on sitting at the small table outside the shop for long but found herself lingering to watch the people before recalling that she was going to need to cover lots of ground today.

Once at the courtyard outside the museum, she could see the vast complex of buildings forming the two main quadrilaterals. She spent some time observing the old architecture and could see why the city officials were considering a grand expansion and remodel over the next decade. It surely needed it, but right now Kat just wanted to get in to see the incredible works of art she had studied in school. Making her way through the archway and into the entrance to pay, she found herself already enthralled. It was difficult to decide where to start, and she was determined to make it as far as possible today. Certainly she'd see the *Mona Lisa* and works depicting Venus and Athena before the day was out.

By noon, Kat had already stood in front of so many amazing paintings, tapestries, and statues. Within short order, she'd been able to locate the restroom and find some lunch, so she was now ready to continue her trek through the seemingly endless treasures. By 4:00 p.m., she was on to the hunt for the sculpture of Cupid and Psyche that she didn't want to miss. Getting some directions from one of the staff, she located the large room that contained the work and entered in.

The moment she got into the room Kat drew in her breath at the sight of the incredible sculpture. It captivated her immediately. For nearly ten minutes, Kat stood to stare at the amazing piece, changing locations several times to catch it from every angle possible. She then pulled out a small drawing pad and pencil from her purse to write down her observations, approximate dimensions, and other impressions.

While Kat was totally immersed in what she was seeing, she sensed that there was someone else studying the piece from behind her. The shadow of movement from behind became the reality of a tall and swarthy man walking to the other side of the sculpture to view the expectant kiss between the lovers depicted in the incredible work of art.

Kat was initially irritated that he was in her line of sight until she took her eyes off the masterpiece to instead focus on the face she saw between the white marble figures. Now that was "art" she thought to herself. With his shoulder-length, chocolate-colored hair pulled back in a ponytail and his dark brown eyes looking at Psyche, he appeared to be in deep concentration. Kat, on the other hand, had totally lost her focus for the statue, having seen this incredibly handsome specimen behind the sculpture.

The man made his way all around the artwork and ended up standing right next to her. Rubbing his chiseled jawline with his hand, he leaned toward her and whispered, "Que beso dulce." Kat had learned enough Spanish in school to know he was referring to the "sweet kiss" of Cupid and Psyche. Trying to appear equally focused on the artwork in front of them, she responded with a simple, "Si." The gentleman didn't seem to need much more than that and appeared ready to move on to the next work. But as he turned to walk away he looked back over his shoulder to ask her—in English this time—if she would accompany him to dinner tonight. Stunned by the abrupt request from the handsome stranger, yet deeply intrigued, Kat repeated herself by saying "Si."

The tall, dark, and handsome man responded by walking back to her and taking her one free hand in his to kiss it while bending at the waist in a bow to her. She wasn't sure what to make of this amazingly romantic fellow. When he straightened up again, he asked, "Do you always talk to strangers when traveling abroad?" Now self-conscious of her quick response to his offer, she began to wonder if she'd made the wrong choice, or at least made herself appear to be a loose woman. The gentleman seemed to recognize her momentary embarrassment and quickly introduced himself. "My name is Juan Diego Alvarez. There, now I am no longer a stranger to you. And what is your name lovely lady?"

She awkwardly blurted out her name. "I'm Katarina Steiner. I'm pleased to meet you, Mr. Alvarez."

She felt quite frozen in place, even while he slowly took the pad of paper from her hand and turned to a blank page. Returning the pad to her, he calmly suggested she write the name of her hotel on the paper so that he could meet her there at 8:00 p.m. to take her to dinner. She dutifully obliged and tore off the page to hand it over to him. He folded the white paper and tucked it into the pocket of his black shirt and proceeded to once again bow and quietly depart from the room.

All alone in the gallery room now, Kat wasn't sure what just happened. She stood there in silence as her mind was racing back over the interaction with the handsome man in black. One thing was certain; she'd suddenly lost all interest in the Louvre and was ready to head back to her hotel room. While her feet ached from walking and standing all day, her head was spinning as she retraced her steps to the exit of the magnificent museum. It was after 5:00 p.m. when she unlocked the door to her hotel room and flopped down on the bed.

CHAPTER 7

Kat woke up startled with a sense of urgency that quickly moved to panic. Having fallen asleep on the bed, she now clutched at her watch to check the time. Oh, thank heavens! It was only 7:00 p.m., she assured herself. With just one hour, she needed to pull herself together, especially in light of the fact that she'd slept in her sundress.

A quick bath was followed by a bit of makeup and a brushing out her long tresses that curled freely below her shoulders. The only thing left was deciding what to wear on this date she was very much looking forward to, despite wondering if she'd made a mistake in agreeing to the meeting. She selected her black leather pants because they accentuated her long legs, especially when wearing heels. Pairing the pants with a shimmery, royal blue, cowl-necked top; big earrings; and plenty of bangles, she was ready to head out the door. Shoving the room key into her purse, she caught a glimpse of herself in the mirror above the dresser and pointed to the image with approval.

Fashionably late at 8:05 p.m., Kat was in the lobby to greet her date who was staring out at the patio through the double doors off the small lobby. Once again, he reached for her hand and kissed it saying, "Buenas tardes, Katarina." She was trying hard to feel every bit of his touch on her hand—from the softness of his lips to the brief brush of facial hair owing to his five o'clock shadow.

"Good evening to you, Mr. Alvarez," responded Kat.

He immediately corrected her by saying, "Please, no formalities tonight. Just call me Juan Diego." In turn, she figured it was time to let him know that she just went by Kat.

He continued to hold onto her long fingers and then stepped back a bit to take her in. Without giving her time to be self-conscious of his gaze, he said, "You look lovely in that shade of blue, Kat." She thanked him and asked him if he was familiar enough with Paris to know where they might have dinner. He responded by asking her how she knew he wasn't from Paris, causing her to smile while trying not to laugh.

"Oh, perhaps it was the fact that you haven't spoken a word of French to me yet!" said Kat. He smiled and went on to tell her that his own hotel concierge had recommended a restaurant a few blocks away from her hotel.

As the two headed out into the warmer than usual evening, Juan Diego offered up his arm for Kat to grab onto. He seemed eager to be her escort, so she obliged by linking her arm with his. The evening stroll started with small talk about the lovely weather, but soon Juan Diego moved on to provide her with some additional information about himself. "I've been in Paris on business these last few days, but that concluded yesterday, so I thought I'd stay a few extra days to enjoy the city before returning home to Mexico." Kat was not at all surprised by the revelation of his country of origin because she had detected his accent, even though he spoke excellent English. He went on to specify that he was

from Baja California and a small town there called Todos
Santos.

As they walked arm in arm, Kat was growing increasingly interested in knowing more about this handsome fellow. She began with, "How is it that you speak such excellent
English?" He responded by telling her that he had attended
graduate school in the United States, Princeton to be exact. She was certainly intrigued about how he ended up
there and was about to inquire further when he turned the
conversation back to her.

"Clearly, you are American," he stated, "but which state
are you from, and what brings you to Paris?"

As she was formulating her thoughts to respond, he
pointed to their restaurant and recommended they get
seated before she answered because he didn't want to miss
a single detail. She followed his lead and soon a gentleman
was asking them if they wanted to dine inside or at one of
the outside tables. Between the two of them, they seemed
to know enough French to figure out what they were being asked and to indicate their preference to dine inside
this evening. Kat had a sense that Juan Diego might be the
type who had a great appreciation for the outdoors, but
she wanted to be a bit more secluded and undistracted this
evening.

Within minutes, they were being seated at a table for
two near the back corner of the restaurant. It was the perfect
location for being out of the way. As they settled in, Juan
Diego asked her if he might order a bottle of wine for the two
of them. Kat was quite up for that, for it seemed there was
no better place for wine than France. The waiter brought a
sweet and silky merlot, along with two small loaves of bread,
while they considered what to order for dinner. The menu
was difficult to decipher, but they decided to indulge in the
chateaubriand for two.

Once the waiter departed, Juan Diego folded his hands in front of his face and sat staring across the table at the beautiful woman he had found in Le Louvre earlier today. Kat could feel his penetrating eyes and knew he was expecting her to tell him all about herself. She began by confirming, "Yes, I am an American from Carmel, California."

Juan Diego dropped his hands to the table and flashed a beautiful smile at her saying, "How convenient!"

Kat was a bit taken back by that comment but kept going. "This trip to Paris is a graduation gift for me, having just spent four years in Los Angeles attending the University of Southern California."

After congratulating her on the achievement, Juan Diego added, "However, USC is not really in southern California. That's where I'm from!"

The conversation was on a roll with the two of them sharing information about themselves. Kat learned that he had studied architecture and building technology in Mexicali, before moving on to Princeton, where he received his master's degree in architecture. Juan Diego learned that she had studied art history, with a particular interest in sculpture. He learned that Kat was an only child, and now orphaned. She learned that he was one of four boys and that his elderly father lived at the family villa with him. They both learned that he was four years older than her, and he now knew that she was headed for Vienna after this part of her vacation in Paris.

As their dinner was arriving at the table, Kat just had to ask, "Is your name one name or two?"

She could tell that he was an amused by her question as he went on to explain, "Actually, my full name is Juan Diego Leonel Alvarez, and I have fewer given names than most of my friends and relatives!" They both got a laugh over that, as he went on to inform her it was therefore not uncommon for family and friends to just call him JD.

He then reached over to touch her hand, and locking eyes with hers, he said, "And you are now a friend." Kat was now connected to her new friend by the touch of his hand on hers and the feeling of falling into his deep brown eyes. The entrancement left her barely able to speak the words, "Espero que si." JD promptly followed up with a reassuring, "No need to simply *hope* so; now you know so."

The walk back to the hotel that night provided the two with a classic Paris evening, twinkling lights and all. They took their time and walked hand in hand, taking turns asking questions about each other. It was on this walk that JD asked Kat to spend the entire day with him the next day as it would be his last day in Paris. She told him she couldn't imagine spending the day without him, knowing it was their last day together.

As they rounded the corner onto the street of her hotel, he stopped to face her. Taking both of her hands in his, he raised them to his lips to kiss her fingers. JD then proceeded to tell her, "I don't want tomorrow to be the last day I ever see you." He asked her to provide him with her address and phone number and promised he would make contact with her when they were both home again. Kat was thrilled to hear this but had lingering doubts about his intentions. She thought perhaps it was the wine and the beautiful Paris nightscape talking but obliged him by writing her contact information on the back of a city map she had stashed away in her purse. To her, this encounter seemed the stuff of fairy tales; though admittedly, it was one that she wanted to believe in.

As they entered the hotel, JD stopped by the front desk to ask the attendant to call a cab for him as his hotel was on the other side of the Seine. He then offered to walk Kat to her room down the hall, to which she agreed. Standing in front of her room, he took the room key from her and opened the door for her. As he handed the key back to her, he put his arm around her waist and drew her to himself. Ever so close now, he thanked her for the evening and told her he'd be back for her by 9:00 a.m. in the lobby. She nodded without saying a word. JD coyly asked, "Will you keep saying 'yes' if I ask to kiss you goodnight?" Kat nodded again, and he pressed his lips to hers, not once but several times before releasing her. And somewhere in between kisses, he whispered to her the very first words she heard from him that day, "Que beso dulce."

As Kat closed and locked the door to her room, she leaned back against it and drew in a long breath and exhaled slowly. She could hardly believe what had just happened to her, a dream date like none other. As she dropped her purse on the chair, she twirled around once and felt like she was walking on air. It was now nearly 11:00 p.m., and though she was tired, she wasn't sure if she'd be able to sleep. However, as she undressed, slipped on her nightgown, and climbed into the comfy bed, she quickly drifted off to a contented sleep knowing she'd see JD again in the morning.

CHAPTER 8

Kat got her 8:00 a.m. wake-up call and then sat up in bed to stretch. With the morning sun already coming through the window of her hotel room, the excitement of what today might hold caused her to throw back the covers to greet the day. She definitely wanted to look her best today, so after plenty of time in the bathroom, she emerged to figure out what to wear. She had brought some turquoise capris with a pretty matching swing-top with cutaway shoulders. Donning the outfit, pulling on her strappy wedge shoes and grabbing her purse, she was ready to head out.

Entering the lobby, she could almost hear her heart beating faster as she spotted JD coming in the front door of the hotel. She didn't think he could be any better looking, but she'd not seen him with his hair falling loose around his face. JD held the door for her saying, "Buenos dias, Katarina," to which she responded, "Good morning to you, JD." Once out in the beautiful sunshine, he took her hand in his. He announced that he needed his morning coffee and that he had seen a café nearby they could walk to. Kat mentioned that she'd had breakfast there the day she met him in the Louvre and that they made a good cup of coffee.

As they walked to the café, JD inquired, "How much do you think we might be able to accomplish today?" She wondered out loud if they might see the Eiffel Tower, the Arch, Notre-Dame, and maybe the museum with sculptures by Rodin. He smiled and said, "My, you are feeling ambitious!"

"Well, admittedly, all that might be too much," Kat answered. But JD liked what he heard and was projecting optimism about the plan as they found an outside table. They ordered some coffee and pastries, and the waiter was off to fetch them.

"JD, tell me more about your business and Todos Santos," Kat requested.

He began by informing her that he was involved in a number of things back home. "I have some acreage that enables me to farm crops and maintain horses." Kat was intrigued by the latter, and he could tell by the "Oh, how wonderful!" that she injected at that point in the conversation. JD was pleased to see her interest because he was an expert horseman and riding truly was his first love. He proceeded to tell her that he'd learned early in life not to depend on one source of income, so he had cultivated several, the largest of which was a cement enterprise he managed out of the free port city of La Paz. That, he told her, was his biggest reason for business travel these days as the international demand was high.

Kat was fascinated by the world he lived in but was also having a hard time imagining Mexico in those terms. She had always thought of the poverty of that nation rather than its enterprise. She pushed through that stereotype to ask him more about the ranch. JD told her, "It's a beautiful spot because it sits just off the beach and includes some private beachfront. And, as you know, I live in the main house there with my only remaining parent, my father. Then, there is

Carmen, who is both my cook and housekeeper. And lastly, I have an overseer of the many acres and the horses, and his name is Bernardo."

Kat expressed her amazement at what sounded like a large estate and told JD, "I just have a small two-bedroom cottage in Carmel." He smiled and told her he knew a bit about property values in the two locations and speculated that they might actually have the same price tag. Of course, Kat knew her small cottage was in one of the most beautiful places in the western part of the United States, yet she was still in awe of the ranch JD had just described.

As they finished up their breakfast, it was easy enough to catch a passing cab to head to the nearest attraction on their list—the Cathedral of Notre-Dame. Kat was very excited to see the edifice. Knowing that most people from Mexico were Roman Catholic, she assumed that it might have some significance to JD that went beyond architecture. The couple sat in the backseat enjoying the brief ride, and eventually, the beautiful French Gothic building came into view. Hopping out of the cab, Kat insisted on paying the driver. JD looked askance but didn't want to argue with his lovely travel companion.

As the two sightseers approached the beautiful cathedral, JD was already commenting on the rose window and flying buttresses. No doubt this was a thrill for an architecture aficionado, but Kat was also taking in the incredible art of it all. They spent the next few hours touring and even climbing the hundreds of steps to the tower. They both found the gargoyles to be a curious touch to a Roman Catholic cathedral. In fact, it was JD who brought it up first, which gave Kat an opening to ask him about his faith. "I presume you think it's odd from your perspective as a Catholic?" inquired Kat.

"I suppose I would, even if I were Catholic," he replied. "However, I'm part of a religious minority in Sur Baja; I'm actually Baptist. There's a story to that; if you're interested, I'll tell you more over dinner at the Eiffel Tower where I've made reservations for us tonight!"

As they finished up at Notre-Dame around 11:30 a.m., JD suggested they'd better catch another cab to the Musée Rodin where they could also find some lunch. Once they arrived there, they decided to grab a bite to eat from a street vendor of sweet and savory crepes. That would hold them through the several hours they would spend at the museum, where Kat was in her element. The two of them enjoyed what they saw inside, as well as in the gardens where JD struck his very best *Thinker* pose for Kat.

As they were well into the afternoon now, they walked to the busy Champs-Elysées to take in the Arc de Triomphe and walk the tree-lined avenue. The two were getting to know Paris a bit better, and also getting to know each other much better. Both seemed to operate at a similar pace and easygoing tempo. Kat sensed the compatibility between the two but was still not sure how to interpret their relationship… or even if they'd still have one after they went their own ways. Nonetheless, for now, the man and the setting made for the ultimate in a romantic vacation.

After mailing a postcard to Barb back in California, their last stop before heading to the Eiffel Tower that evening was a little boutique in the shopping district. JD was more than patient to sit in a chair and pass judgment as Kat tried on dresses. She was determined to select something to take home with her, perhaps something that JD might like to see her wearing.

After modeling three dresses that he seemed to think were pretty enough, she walked out in dress number four—

a short, strapless, bustier-style dress with a large red and black flower pattern on a white background. It was something that accentuated her lovely legs, bust, and neckline, and she was certainly tall enough to get away with the big print. JD responded immediately when she came out of the dressing room with "Que bella!" He stood up, took her hand, and twirled her around once while looking her over. Kat decided that if it warranted "How beautiful!" from JD, it seemed this was the dress!

After Kat bought the dress, the couple hailed a cab to head back over the river to the Eiffel Tower. It was late enough that the lights in the city were appearing, and the tower was lit up when they came within sight. JD took her hand as they got out of the cab, and in that moment, Kat realized how much of her day she had spent smiling. In fact, she thought she might be the happiest woman on earth this evening.

As the two walked toward the base of the tower, JD stopped in its shadow and turned toward her. Without any hesitation, he took her face in his hands and kissed her like she'd never been kissed before. When he stopped, she was left staring into his brown eyes that twinkled in the lights around them. She whispered quietly, "I know it's not my birthday, so what was that for?"

JD smiled as he continued to hold her face close to his and said, "I just don't want you to forget this moment, but more importantly, I don't want you to forget me." All she could say was, "As if." The two held each other tightly for several minutes before collecting themselves to go up to the restaurant for dinner.

The dinner and the view out of the window, as well as the man in front of her, were exquisite, and Kat was enjoying the whole experience. JD was explaining to her what his plans were upon his return to Mexico. Then he began asking her about where she'd being staying, her Austrian relatives, and other details about her visit there next week. It seemed very important to him that he know when she would be back in Carmel. "I'll be flying back into San Francisco airport on Saturday, July 5 and then driving the two hours home. I should be home no later than 8:00 p.m. that night," she estimated.

All this talk gave Kat some sense of optimism about the possibility that she might at least hear from JD again. It wasn't that he'd made any promises, but at least he seemed to be tracking the fact that they'd both be back on the same coast by early July.

As they were finishing up the main course, JD laid his hand out on the table palm up. With his brown eyes searching her dark blue eyes, he was signaling his request for her hand. She obliged, and he held on while asking, "How is it that such a beautiful woman like you would not be spoken for? Was there... is there someone?"

Kat shifted a bit in her chair and responded, "Yes, there was someone once, or so I thought. I dated a guy in college during my junior year. I really can't say that I was in love with him because the relationship ended somewhat abruptly when my parents died. He graduated that same week, a year before me."

JD continued to press her asking, "This guy has no name? Are you avoiding saying his name because you still have feelings for him?"

Kat looked surprised by the question, even to the point of taking a second to assess her feelings, then added, "His name is Jason, and I'd rather not talk about him. That's past, and I want to be present with you. Besides, I could be asking what's a handsome man like you doing unattached at age 25?"

JD smiled, lifted her hand to his lips, and kissed her fingertips before releasing her hand. He finally answered by admitting, "Though I've enjoyed the company of various ladies over the years, I've been largely committed to my work and family obligations. I suppose none have held my attention for very long."

When the dessert arrived, Kat took the opportunity to change the subject to ask JD about his faith. He told her that his grandparents had lived and worked in Texas when they were young and that was where they became believers. JD went into a lengthy explanation of this family's return to Mexico and subsequent involvement in what eventually led to the National Baptist Convention in Mexico. He also mentioned that his father was still hopeful that the Mexican government would someday recognize the denomination and, despite his poor health, was active in the movement to see that happen.

With that as background, JD went on to express his own faith to Kat. "I came to faith in Jesus Christ as a young boy and was even baptized on the stretch of beach that now belongs to me. My values, and I hope my behaviors, are built on the Rock—Jesucristo." With that, he stopped to ask her, "Are you uncomfortable with the discussion and knowing this about me?"

Kat looked him in the eyes and told him, "It would be impossible for me to be uncomfortable with spiritual kin because I, too, know Christ as my personal Lord and Savior." JD again took her hand across the table and smiled.

After a wonderful dinner together, it seemed the dread of having to say goodbye was starting to set in for both of them. They lingered as long as they could, feeding the last bites of their shared dessert to each other across the table. As they arose to leave, JD reached for her hand again and held onto it all the way to the cab. Once they were in the backseat of the vehicle and headed for her hotel, he put his arm around her, and Kat rested her head on his shoulder. They continued their conversation in low tones as he played with her hair with his hand. To be sure, they were friends, but it was clear to both of them that there was an attraction and a growing bond, despite the fact that they had known each other for only a short time.

JD asked the cab driver to wait for him as he walked Kat to her hotel room again this night. She was not looking forward to saying goodbye, yet she was eagerly looking forward to being on the receiving end of his kisses. She had definitely concluded that nobody could possibly be a better kisser than JD. He didn't disappoint her, kissing her repeatedly while holding her shoulders in his strong hands. She wanted it to go on forever, but he stopped and wished her the best for the remainder of her vacation. He also thanked her for being willing to say "si" to his offer in the museum the day before, speculating aloud, "How sad it would have been had I missed the opportunity to know you." Kat reminded him that it took his bold request to bring them together, and with a twinkle in her eye, she thanked him for his kisses. She figured it might buy her one more, and she was right. JD wrapped his arms around her and kissed her deeply one last time before turning to walk back to the lobby and out to the waiting cab.

CHAPTER 9

With several more days left in Paris, Kat returned to her list of things she had wanted to see. Several of them were scratched off from her full day of touring with JD, though there were still many museums of art she wanted to visit. She would accomplish it all, but each passing day reminded her of how much she longed for the company she had on her first days there.

The day soon arrived for her to catch her two-hour flight to Vienna. As she brought her bag to the front desk to check out, the clerk took her key, processed her payment, and pointed her to the waiting cab outside the glass doors of the lobby. As she headed out the door, she heard the clerk shout "Mademoiselle!" She turned around to see him reaching out to her with a piece of paper in his outstretched hand. He seemed to be apologizing, though she wasn't sure what he was saying. With his limited English skills, he blurted out, "Today, this for you!" She thanked him and opened the envelope to find a telegram. Her heart was pounding as she saw it was from Mexico. It simply read: *Have fun in Vienna. Good to be home but thinking of you day and night. JD*

As Kat slipped into the backseat of the cab, she reread the telegram several times. While she was looking forward to seeing her relatives, she knew she'd be distracted over the next week. She confirmed in her mind that she would need to keep quiet about JD and place her full attention on her grandparents and other family there.

Before long, she was boarding her flight and looking at the brochure about the hotel where the travel agent had placed her in Vienna. It looked beautiful and was right on the Ringstrasse very close to the state opera. She was definitely looking forward to the arts, culture, and music that Vienna had to offer. Later in the flight, she pulled out an old photograph she had of her grandparents. It had been several years since the picture was taken, and since Kat had seen them. She hoped she'd recognize them when she saw them again.

As the plane neared Vienna, the wing dipped a bit as the pilot made a turn. It was enough that even from her aisle seat, Kat could see the city coming into view. From the air, the glorious city looked flat and unassuming; still she knew better and was looking forward to visiting the palaces, cathedrals, theaters, and cafés. Though she had not been in Vienna since she was 14 years old, she remembered that the city was full of beautiful outdoor sculpture. Such a tiny country but carefully rebuilt to what was now the crossroads of central Europe.

Within the hour, she was picking up her bag, hailing a cab to her hotel, and making contact with her grandparents so that they could connect for dinner in the city. Kat was hoping to treat them to several outings while she was in town. They would no doubt be wonderful tour guides since this had always been their home. Her grandma and grandpa Steiner were very hospitable people who were disappointed that she had chosen to stay in a hotel rather than in their small apartment. However, Kat felt it was best for all concerned.

Upon checking in at the beautiful hotel, Kat was already impressed with how much more sophisticated she felt the city had become in just the few years since she last saw it. The cab ride had also reminded her of how clean the city always appeared. Kat wondered how much of her Austrian heritage had influenced her love of the arts, music, and even her desire to keep her surroundings neat and tidy wherever she was. Clearly, the people of Austria embraced all three, and despite the fact that she spoke very little German, she felt like she fit right in. The bellhop appeared to think so too because he first spoke to her in German while helping her with her bag, before realizing she was American.

Getting settled in her room, she made a call to her grandparents who were thrilled that she had arrived safely. Margrit insisted that Kat come to their apartment for dinner, letting her know that her Aunt Annika had also been invited. Kat made arrangements to be at their place by 6:00 p.m. to spend the evening with them.

Kat was pleased to hear that she'd have some time to get to know her aunt a bit better. Annika had been a bit of a family mystery though Kat knew she was also an artist. The only other thing she really knew of Aunt Annika was that she had married a German man when she was in her early thirties. As the story went, within six months of being married, it came to light that the man was already married with a family he had abandoned back in Germany. After a quick annulment, Annika had remained unmarried ever since. Kat recalled hearing her parents talk about Annika's bitterness and distrust of men from that point. However, not long before her death, her mother had mentioned that she'd heard Annika was "in a relationship" with another artist in town. Whatever was going on, Kat was willing to spend many evenings learning more about the family and, thereby, her own history.

CHAPTER 10

After taking a cab across town, Kat pushed the buzzer and was soon being greeted by her grandmother's hug, with her grandfather standing right behind her awaiting his own hug. Kat did recognize them and instantly realized how almost impossible it is for blood relations not to, despite the years. Margrit and Arne were elderly, but even at their age, they appeared to be in good health.

No sooner had the hugs broken up than Kat saw Aunt Annika coming out from the small kitchen while still wiping her hands on a dish towel. Annika was Johannes Steiner's older sister, and Kat was struck by how similar their builds were, both tall and thin. However, Annika's hair was now silver, and she wore her long hair up in a French twist. The two hugged, and Annika then stepped back to look at Kat and exclaim, "Oh, little girl, how beautifully you have grown up!"

The dinner fare was simple and tasty. Kat had recalled her grandmother to be a good cook, especially with desserts. She wasn't disappointed when Margrit brought out her own version of Sachertorte with whipped cream. The four had a great time talking about the days of Kat's childhood, and she learned more tidbits about her parents that she didn't know. Though there was clearly sadness over their collective loss, tonight was a great celebration of the lives of Johannes and Liesl.

Inevitably, the conversation turned to Kat and her plans now that she had graduated. She actually sensed an unspoken desire on the part of her elders for her to consider moving to Austria. Perhaps, she thought, they may have wondered if she was lonely and in need of family. Kat was delicate in choosing her words as she didn't want to offend her relatives. It wasn't that she didn't like Austria, and she had looked forward to the visit. However, Kat had never thought of herself as anything but a red-blooded American girl. She loved the United States and California in particular. In fact, she was looking forward to casting her first vote in the upcoming presidential election for a man from her own state.

Kat informed her family members that she would be returning to California but was still considering her options for life and work in Carmel. She even tossed out the idea of opening her own studio and perhaps teaching art. They seemed satisfied with that but reminded her that Austria was "home to art" as far as they were concerned.

With that, Kat inquired of them, "Might I take you all to the Vienna State Opera house later this week to see the performance of La Bohéme?" All three were game to do that, so Kat agreed to pick up the tickets and arrange for the evening.

By the time Kat arrived back at her hotel that evening, it was nearly 10:00 p.m. Passing through the lobby and up the elevator to her room, she entered exhausted and ready for a good night sleep. Catching a glimpse of something on the small round table in her room, she dropped off her purse and walked further into the room to see a vase full of beautiful red-tipped yellow roses. Her heart skipped a beat as she saw the small white envelope tucked into the arrangement. Plucking it out and opening the envelope, she slowly pulled out the typed message that read: *Kat—May you enjoy these flowers for the time you are in Vienna. And may they also daily remind you of me. JD*

CHAPTER 11

The time Kat had with her grandparents was spent visiting St. Stephen's Cathedral, Schönbrunn Palace, and many other city sights. It was more difficult for the elderly couple to keep up on some of the visits, but that just meant Kat had more time to linger in front of sculptures, ceramics, and paintings. Her grandparents were also quite content to sit for long periods of time while Kat wandered down cobblestone side streets to peek into shops. And for the entire trip, the weather had cooperated with sunny days and mild temperatures, making the hanging flower baskets around town pop with vibrant color.

The week in Vienna passed quickly, but Kat got out and about with Aunt Annika to visit art galleries, museums, and street fairs. In Annika, Kat felt she had found a relative who understood her love of artistic expression. Kat also learned that Annika was no longer seeing the starving artist her mother had mentioned. That matter came up in a conversation she had while seated outside of Café Central with her aunt as they lingered over cups of rich coffee.

"So, Auntie, I hadn't planned on mentioning this to anyone here, but I met a handsome stranger in Paris who was very intriguing. We only had two days together, and I hardly know what to make of the whole encounter," Kat admitted.

Annika's eyebrows were raised, and her eyes almost had a look of fear in them. "Young lady, you should probably just forget about this man, for very likely he's forgotten about you. Oh, not because you aren't beautiful, smart, and kind— because you are all those things. Forget about him because men don't have much of sense of anyone else who isn't in their presence. It's like the saying... how does that go... ah yes, out of sight, out of mind."

Kat didn't want to believe that about JD and countered Annika's cynicism by telling her that JD had sent a telegram and even had flowers sent to her hotel. Waiting for her aunt's reaction to the additional information, Annika took her time sipping coffee before responding by patting Kat's hand and saying, "Dear girl, they all pay attention for a time, but who knows what may have caught his attention by now. You should count this meeting in Paris as a fleeting gift but don't expect anything more to come of it."

Kat decided to be more daring in her challenge to Annika by asking about the man she had been seeing. Annika didn't seem challenged at all by the question, calmly responding, "Oh, Max? Well, that was short-lived and hardly romantic, Kat. He was about ten years older than me and was only looking for a nursemaid in his old age. Like your young man, he sent me flowers once, though I don't know how he could have afforded them. Once he realized I wasn't simply going to move in with him and start cooking for him and paying his bills, he seemed to be on to the next thing. That's the problem with men, Kat; they always seem to be chasing the next thing. Once upon a time, even I was the next thing, only to find out I was really just another thing."

Kat felt badly that she'd brought Annika back through past heartache and said so. Annika once again patted her hand and said, "Don't worry about me, young lady. I'll be fine; I just don't want you to get your heart broken."

All in all, the days in Vienna had been delightful, but when Kat returned to her hotel each night, she looked at the beautiful roses and pined for JD's company. It had been more than a week since she'd seen him, yet the memory of his dreamy brown eyes were a constant reminder as she drifted off to sleep each night. But memories couldn't replace being held in his strong arms, or being over the moon with his kisses.

After goodbyes over her last family dinner the night before, Kat was packed up and ready to catch her cab to the airport that morning. As she was preparing to leave her hotel room, she thought she should probably place her fading roses in the trash and empty the vase, but she couldn't bring herself to do it. Leaving everything as it was, she brought her own suitcase down to the lobby where the bellhop grabbed it to carry out to the cab. Kat checked out at the front desk, mailed a postcard to Larry, and hurried out to catch her ride to the airport, but not without stopping to take in a deep breath of the lovely Vienna morning air. The trip had been good for her soul; still she was now ready to get home to Carmel.

The trip home, with an unexpected delay in Chicago, meant Kat didn't arrive at the long-term parking for her car outside of the San Francisco airport until about 7:00 p.m. that night. As she put her things in the trunk and settled into the driver's seat for the additional two hours of travel home, it seemed as though thoughts of JD were now constantly before her. All she knew was that she hoped to hear from him this week, for now he knew she'd be stateside again.

CHAPTER 12

Kat had gotten a good night sleep in her own bed, so she woke up refreshed and ready to greet this Sunday morning, July 6. She decided to head up the road to the small Bible church her parents had been a part of when they moved to Carmel. Though Kat figured she'd check into a few churches within a reasonable driving radius, she thought she'd start with the one she'd attended a few times when she was home from college for holidays. This little church had also been so supportive of her during her loss last year, even memorializing her parents by planting a tree on their grounds in their honor.

Driving up the highway to the small church, her mind strained to recall the last time she was there. She'd not even been there for Easter services this year as she had chosen to go home over the break with Barb Beasley instead. As she searched her memory, it finally dawned on her that it had been over six months since she'd attended the little church. During that stretch of time, she continued to get their occasional mailings and had noticed that a pulpit search had finally resulted in a new pastor this past spring. Kat was eager to hear him preach.

Greeted heartily at the door of the church by some friends of her parents, Kat settled into a pew with a few of them. She felt very welcomed and thoroughly enjoyed the Sunday sermon by Pastor Keith Summers. He spoke on Christ as the one foundation, immovable and knowable through the Word of God. It was a sermon that was deep and wide in its use of scripture and ended with a clear call for the people of the Lord to cling to the Cross even while others chose to wander in search of "new thought." Kat was so impressed that she determined at that moment that this would be her church home. She also wished that her parents could see what had become of the small congregation, for she was sure they'd be pleased that the flock seemed to have found a good undershepherd.

As she contemplated her parents, she was once again conscience of the empty space she felt in her life. She wished so much she could talk with them about her next steps and maybe even tell them about her trip and how good it was to see the family in Austria again.

Feeling a bit sorry for herself, Kat found herself driving home while humming the old hymn the congregation had sung after the sermon, "The Solid Rock." Remembering that all the verses spoke of Christ being the Rock even when all other things seem stormy and difficult, Kat prayed for that kind of confidence in the Lord.

CHAPTER 13

Many days had now passed since her return from vacation, and still Kat had heard nothing from JD—no call, no letter, no flowers, nothing. She had sent him a postcard of the beautiful white sand beach of Carmel to thank him for the flowers, but soon the days turned into weeks. And though they were only 1400 miles apart, she felt as though he was half a world away. Even the words of jaded Aunt Annika were beginning to ring in her ears. Could it be that it had simply been a romantic fling to him, she wondered. But then, why his insistence that she not forget him? Had he so quickly moved on to "the next thing?" Perhaps she too had not held his attention.

Kat tried not to dwell on the silence from JD and instead kept reminding herself to move forward with life. She had even spent most of the month looking for some commercial space where she might open a studio. Coming across a newspaper photo of a small gallery for rent in Seaside, she had contacted the owner in order to view the space. As she headed up the road to make the appointment, Kat turned off the radio and drove in silence, something she'd not done in quite a while. Another thing happened that wasn't common to her; she found herself tearing up. Sending up a prayer for inner peace was the only thing she knew to do at this point. While she was at it, she also asked the Lord to release her from the memories and the budding feelings she had for JD.

As Kat pulled up to the storefront, she could see a tall gentleman in a suit waiting patiently just inside the door. She assumed it was the owner and pulled out of her shirt pocket the note upon which she had written his name. Repeating "Jim Dixon" in a whisper to herself, she got out of the car to greet him. The sandy-haired Jim looked up from the papers he held in his hand and greeted Kat with this free hand. He appeared a bit caught off guard by Kat and that made her wonder what he had expected of his prospective renter.

"I appreciate your taking the time to show me the place," Kat injected.

Setting his documents down, Jim responded with, "No problem, you're the first to call to inspect the space since I ran the ad. I hope it fits your needs. I'd like to see the place active again."

As Jim showed her the space in front, it appeared to have been used for art classes, and there was lots of shelving, which Kat assumed had been used for supplies. As they made their way to the back of the shop, Kat was surprised to find two pottery wheels and a kiln. "So this was a ceramics studio?" she asked. Jim indicated that it was, but that his previous renter had been so far in arrears in rent that he refused to let the wheels out of the building as he might have to sell them to recover some of his losses. Kat was intrigued as she thought she'd love to get her hands on all of that equipment and felt it might be the edge she needed to make something of her business endeavor.

After seeing the place, Kat shook Jim's hand and took his business card. She let him know that she liked the place but wanted to take a look at one other prospect this week. She promised to get back to him one way or the other by the end of the week. Jim seemed almost a bit too eager to hear from her again...and she wasn't sure it had anything to do with the rental space.

CHAPTER 14

As Kat dressed for church on Sunday, she found herself
looking forward to going, yet somewhat dreading attending
alone. She had to admit that this life after graduation had
definitely diminished her social contacts and increased her
loneliness. But Kat was an unusual sort of artist, left-brain
dominant, linear, and logical. Though immensely talented
in her artistic expression, she also wasn't the emotive and
outwardly expressive type that she'd found to be more typical of artists. In fact, she'd sometimes wondered if there was
something wrong with her in that regard. In any case, her
rational thinking usually won the day and that would be the
case this Sunday as well as she drove herself to church.

Parking the car and walking through the breezeway of
the church, Kat shook hands with the Sunday greeters, a
sweet elderly couple. As she entered the lobby, her eyes
locked onto a familiar face that was out of place. Walking
toward her with a big smile and arms wide open was Jason
Gabriel whom she hadn't seen in over a year. "Kat Steiner,
how the heck are you? I thought I'd drive down to surprise
you, though I wasn't sure if you were still attending here,"
exclaimed Jason.

"Wow, I am surprised, Jason! It's good to see you, and to have someone to sit with in church this morning," responded Kat. The two hugged and soon found empty space in one of the rear pews.

Both Kat and her old flame had a hard time concentrating on the service due to the desire to talk. In fact, as the last hymn was announced, Jason leaned over to whisper in her ear, "Let's beat the crowd to lunch by leaving now!" The two made a graceful exit but only because they were so far back that most didn't notice their early departure.

Once in the parking lot, Kat asked Jason to follow her to a local restaurant where they could get caught up. As Kat got into her car and started down the road, her mind was racing back through the events of her junior year when she and Jason were "an item." It had been a whirlwind year as Kat had taken a heavy academic load in the fall when they met in the library one stormy weather evening. Jason had been the prime mover in the relationship, introducing himself and asking her lots of questions about herself that evening. As their conversation continued, they decided they needed to move to a place with fewer people so as not to be a distraction to others. Clearly, it was a night in which neither one of them would get much studying done. Jason had walked her back to her dorm in the pouring rain, under his university varsity jacket that he used as shelter for the two of them.

Kat recalled Jason's quick wit, handsome features, and athletic build. It turned out that Jason was on the university's water polo team and was, therefore, pretty busy too. Kat attended some of his games, and the two were getting to know each other better by the end of the season. However, the relationship was interrupted by both Christmas and the fact that Kat had been spotted on campus by a New York modeling agency representative who wanted Kat to fly out to the city and meet with her boss.

The brief interlude with the agency kept Kat out of school during winter quarter as she toyed with the idea of professional modeling by spending three weeks in several cities in Italy on a shoot and walking in a fashion show in Rome. The agency may have regretted sending her on the trip because what Kat learned in that experience was that her parents were right; modeling was no life at all. While there was no doubt that Kat was a striking beauty who photographed very well, she was appalled by what she found in the industry that was trying desperately to change its image. The fact that the agency head informed her that she needed to shed 10 pounds helped her understand why the other models she met were starving themselves of food, while feeding themselves drugs instead.

Returning to school in the spring, Kat and Jason seemed to pick up where they left off. Having more time for each other, she thought she might be falling for him just as he was getting ready to graduate and return to the Sacramento area to find work. Then it happened. She got the call from the state police about the fatal accident involving her parents, and like so many other things in her life, Jason just seemed to simply fade into the background of life.

Pulling into a parking space right next to hers, Jason jumped out of the car and came around to meet Kat. As they walked into the restaurant, Jason was already asking her about her senior year and how she was getting along in life. She wondered what he was up to as well, remembering that he was a business major who thought he might like to find work in the banking industry after graduation. They found a booth and were off to the races getting caught up after their time apart.

CHAPTER 15

For the next several weeks, Jason called Kat regularly and even sent her some of her favorite perfume in the mail. On one very early August morning, they met in San Francisco for a Saturday of shopping, a visit to the aquarium, and dinner. Their long-distance relationship was not going to stop them from getting reacquainted, though they would be hampered by his work schedule during the week.

Meeting Jason early in the day, they had coffee and mapped out their strategy, which would put them at Alioto's on Fisherman's Wharf for a wonderful dinner after a day of fun. Jason had called ahead to make sure they had a window seat reservation, and between breakfast and dinner, there would be plenty of time to talk about what was going on in their lives.

After graduation, Jason had landed an entry level job with a Federal Intermediate Credit Bank in Sacramento. While he was glad to have the job, he confided in Kat that he wasn't all that interested in the work and even less than satisfied with his boss. Given that, Jason seemed more interested in what Kat was doing with her art and the studio. It was over dinner that he also admitted to the fact that she'd been living in his head for the last year and that he'd missed spending time with her.

"Kat," Jason explained, "I have to admit that the death of your parents at a time when my own parents were so excited about my graduation really made it hard for me to know how I could help. I hoped the flowers I sent to the memorial service telegraphed my concern."

"Oh, certainly, Jason," Kat assured him.

Jason continued with, "Many times I thought about coming back to campus last year to visit you, but quite honestly, it was all I could do to get through the job search and this first year on the new job." Reaching over to take her hand, Jason confessed, "I really was at a loss at the time about how I could support you, but that didn't keep me from thinking about you."

"I understand, Jason. Most people weren't sure what to say to me during that time. I think people want to make it better in such circumstances, yet they know they can't make it better. It's good to know you didn't forget me, and I'm glad we've reconnected," responded Kat.

As their all-day date came to a close and they realized it was time to go their separate ways, Kat reached for the bill on the table and slipped her credit card into the tray. Jason didn't argue with her because they both knew he wasn't exactly pulling down big money on his job.

As they walked out to their cars under the star-studded night sky, Jason stopped Kat from getting into hers so he could put his arms around her waist. Kat put her arms around his neck, and they talked softly about when they might see each other again. Though they made no specific plans, Jason promised to call her again the coming week. As he leaned toward her, Jason reminded her that it had been over a year since he'd kissed her, and that he had missed doing so. He went on to tell her that he hoped they'd be seeing more of each other in the near future, and with that he kissed her goodbye.

Driving home that warm summer night, Kat began reviewing the events of the day in her mind and that wonderful parting kiss from Jason. However, she couldn't escape the fact that she'd not mentioned anything about her time in Paris. Then again, she thought to herself, why would Jason need to know anything about her encounter with someone she'd never see again? In the same moment, she was reminded of that someone; she turned on the car radio only to hear Hall and Oates singing "Wait for Me."

CHAPTER 16

On a mid-August morning, Kat had planned on sleeping in but awoke to the phone ringing insistently by her bedside at 8:00 a.m. Reaching across her pillow, she mustered up her best "Hello," only to hear JD's voice saying her name. She sat straight up in her bed and eagerly responded with, "Oh, JD, it's good to hear from you."

He paused for just a second or two and then launched into a series of apologies that Kat was mentally wading through when he finally came to the reason for his call. "Kat, I've not been able to contact you because of a very serious family situation that took place the day you were traveling back home last month. It's 9:00 a.m. here, and I apologize for calling so early in the morning, but this is the first opportunity I've had to make a call outside the country. I hope you can forgive me. I want you to know the reason I couldn't call; however, it's not something I can discuss over the phone. I'm calling to ask you to be patient and understanding and to assure you that I will make contact again tomorrow."

Kat was so confused by his veiled messages, but wanting to trust JD, she responded with a simple, "Of course, I

look forward to talking again tomorrow then." JD said his
goodbyes, and Kat slowly hung up the phone.

Heart pounding and now sitting on the edge of her bed,
Kat wondered, what could have happened? She knew so
very little about JD's family, and she was also concerned
about whether or not JD himself was okay. In that moment,
she felt completely helpless, so she sent up a prayer for
her friend and his family. Yes, she had almost abandoned
any chance that she might be anything more than a friend
to JD, but she appreciated his call and the opportunity to
intercede in prayer for his situation.

Dressing for the day and having her coffee on the patio,
she stared out at the ocean in confusion this morning. But
one thing she was not confused about was the fact that
she was ready to call Jim Dixon and rent the studio. She
had decided to turn the front of the space into a gallery for
artists to consign their work. In addition to the gallery, she'd
use the back of the space to take on a few students and
create her own art. Kat secretly hoped that all of her efforts
might someday lead to breaking into the art collection and
auction world. For the last several years, Kat had dreamt
of establishing a US version of Sotheby's or Christie's. But
right now, she'd be satisfied just to have a place to do her
own work, which just wasn't possible in the small cottage
by the sea.

At 10:00 a.m., she called Jim to tell him she'd like to rent
the studio on the terms they had discussed and was even
willing to purchase the pottery wheels. Jim seemed very
pleased and asked Kat to meet him at a restaurant near the
studio for lunch to seal the deal. "Sure, I'll meet you there at
noon, though I will not be able to join in the feeding frenzy
as I've got so much to do today," responded Kat. Jim seemed
to brush off the notion, insisting that buying her a lunch

was something he wanted to do. "You are one tenant I'd like to get to know better," said Jim. Kat figured she'd have to be firm with Jim when she met him face-to-face. After all, she thought, this was strictly business.

Meeting Jim at noon at the crowded eatery in Seaside was not something Kat was looking forward to, but she showed up on time, spotted Jim in a booth, and made her way to the table. Jim was quite chipper and started making small talk, even asking her if she'd ever eaten there before. She was in no mood for this. "No, and that will have to wait until another day, Jim. Seriously, I'm here to sign the lease, give you a check, and pick up the keys." Jim was taken aback by Kat's direct approach and didn't try to make another run at the matter. Within 10 minutes, they had concluded the business, and Jim handed over the keys to her new enterprise. "All the best, Miss Steiner," said Jim as she gathered up her things and departed. Kat felt a bit guilty about giving Jim the cold shoulder, but she really wasn't the least bit interested in a social relationship with her landlord. Besides, she had to admit to herself that she was having a hard enough time sorting out her feelings about Jason's interest in rekindling their relationship, not to mention the faint spark of hope that had come with JD's call.

CHAPTER 17

The morning brought another beautiful day on the ocean. Kat was up early to get in a walk along the beach and collect some driftwood for another art project she was contemplating. Once she arrived back home for her second cup of coffee, she was torn between staying by the phone to take JD's call and tackling all the things on her "to do" list. While she was cleaning up and putting on something a bit nicer than her beach walking shorts and a tee shirt, she decided to make a run up to Seaside to at least take inventory of the rental space. She'd need to make a list of the things she needed to buy, repair, and install. Though she was pretty handy, she had already resigned herself to bringing in some professionals to do some of the work she had in mind.

Having started so early, Kat was able to make it to the studio and back with a side trip to the hardware store to pick up a few items. She made it home by noon and figured she'd spend the afternoon working on that new art project after she made herself some lunch. After lunch, Kat would also take time out for her 1:00 p.m. appointment with a contractor who was coming by to give her an estimate on some of the remodeling work she wanted to do on the cottage.

As she was wrapping up her walk-through and discussion with the contractor, Kat noticed a car parked on the street outside her big picture window in the front of the cottage. She had seen the contractor pull into her driveway in his pickup truck, so she knew it wasn't his vehicle. The city ordinances didn't allow for street parking in order to discourage beachgoers from filling up the surrounding neighborhood. However, she dismissed it for now, thinking it might be a visitor for her neighbor who often held frequent Bunco parties with her friends.

Saying goodbye to the contractor at the door, Kat returned to the back of the cottage where she left her project spread out on the kitchen counter. Just as she made her way to the kitchen to begin organizing her supplies, the doorbell rang. Kat was beginning to wonder if there were solicitors making rounds in the neighborhood. With an impatient sigh, she put down the tool she was working with and went to the door. As she passed by the picture window, she noticed the vehicle was gone from the street. Opening the door, Kat audibly gasped at the sight of JD standing on her porch holding a beautiful bouquet of flowers. It was all she could do to hold back tears, but she certainly couldn't hold back the hugs. He opened his arms wide to receive her even while juggling the flowers behind her back.

"JD, it's so great to see you, but what are you doing here?"

Stepping back he responded, "I told you I'd make contact today. And I could certainly put up with more of that kind of contact with you!" All of a sudden, Kat was self-conscious about how messy she looked, while explaining that she thought he'd make contact in the form of another phone call. "I wanted it to be a surprise!" explained JD. "Now, are you going to keep me standing outside all day?" he inquired.

As Kat invited JD into her home, he was already explaining that he'd been a bit concerned that she might be entertaining another man when he pulled up in his rental car to see a truck parked in her driveway. Kat put her hands on her hips and looked over at him with a frown—until she realized he was serious. "Oh, that was a contractor I was talking to about getting some work done on the place. Hardly entertaining!" JD looked relieved and went on to explain that he'd parked and walked on the beach while waiting for the truck to depart. With more than a passing curiosity, she asked, "Why? Were you worried?"

With that, JD set the flowers down on a nearby table and pulled Kat to himself and kissed her. Then he began tracing her full lips with his index finger, saying, "Yes...yes, I was worried that you might have given up on me. And I wouldn't blame you if you had."

Kat looked into his deep brown eyes and whispered, "Friends don't give up on friends, now do they?" JD just smiled and asked her if she liked the flowers. "I love flowers, JD, and these are beautiful...as were the ones you sent to my hotel in Vienna nearly two months ago." Realizing that statement sounded a bit accusatory, she quickly followed up with, "Now, do you want to tell me what's been going on? It must be something big, in light of the fact that you felt the need to call on me in person with an explanation."

Kat pulled a pitcher of lemonade from her refrigerator, grabbed two glasses, and invited JD to sit out on the porch with her. They remained there for a long time as JD explained to her that his younger brother, Antonio, who was a student at the Autonomous University of Baja California in Mexicali, had been picked up by the authorities and charged with drug running. JD went on to detail the cryptic call he had received last month from his jailed brother, who proclaimed his innocence and was pleading for help. Having attending the same university as an undergraduate, JD knew the city well. He also knew his brother well enough to know Antonio wasn't the type to be involved in illegal activities, so he immediately departed for Mexicali. Unfortunately, it turned out not to be a simple case of mistaken identity but a full-blown shakedown of the family. JD had remained in Mexicali for a week to negotiate for what amounted to a ransom to spring his brother from the prison. It was apparent that the authorities were on the take, as they knew the family had money.

Kat was stunned by this revelation, but JD wasn't finished. He went on to say, "Kat, while all this was going on, I received word from my housekeeper, Carmen, that my father had experienced a heart attack and was near death in the local hospital. I was delayed by the police, who didn't release my brother for several more days, and it was during that time that our father passed away." JD was certain that his father's heart was simply not able to withstand the strain of the situation involving Antonio that he could do nothing about. JD described his father as frail and wheelchair bound, so now Kat understood that such a stressful event might be too much for his father to bear.

As JD laid out the details of what had transpired in his life over the last several weeks, Kat could see it had taken a toll on him too. He looked weary and deeply saddened by the situation. Though one of the youngest in his family, he seemed to carry the weight of responsibility for his family. That was something she didn't realize or understand, but she certainly understood the loss of a parent. After the entire story came out, she stood up and walked to the back of his chair, leaned over, and put her soft, slender arms around his neck. As tears rolled down her face, she whispered in his ear, "I know what it's like to be without parents, and I wish I could have been there for you. I was praying for you though."

JD stood up and drew her close as the couple hugged each other for a long time. With a slight crack in his voice, he finally spoke saying, "Through it all, never a day went by that I didn't think of how you might be upset that I didn't call or write. I was being followed, and my calls were being monitored in Mexicali. My lawyer was receiving hang-up calls late at night, and even driving home with my brother required a paid and armed escort just to get out of town safely. On top of that, we had a burial to confront when we got home. That ended up being very low-key due to the increased concerns around security of other traveling family members. I hope you can now understand why you didn't hear from me."

Kat told JD she certainly understood, though she admitted to thinking that perhaps their time in Paris had been nothing more than a romantic encounter. Now that she knew what he'd been up against, she felt a mixture of deep sadness for him, but also expressed her relief that he hadn't forgotten her. With his arms still around her waist, JD raised one hand to her chin to position her lips for one more kiss. This time, it was his turn to say, "As if."

CHAPTER 18

The two had talked late into the afternoon when Kat finally got around to telling JD about the business deal she had closed earlier in the day. He promptly asked, "Well, can we go see your studio, which also gives me a good excuse to take you to dinner tonight?" That sounded like a great plan to Kat, so the two headed off to Seaside in JD's rental car.

As he drove, he explained to her that he'd started out early this morning to drive to La Paz to catch a plane to Los Angeles, with a connecting flight to the smaller airport in Monterey. Kat asked a question that she wasn't sure she really wanted to know the answer to but felt she must ask. "When do you have to return home?" JD indicated that he had to leave in the morning to pass through L.A. again, with a few hours there to meet a potential business client for lunch before heading back home. As he finished telling her, he looked over to see her countenance fall over the news of his departure the next day.

"You know I don't like to make you unhappy, but I must admit that pretty little pout of yours is as sexy as it gets," said JD with a smile. Kat reached over to give him a shove even as she was blushing.

"I feel like I just got you back, and now you tell me you're leaving again," she whined. He then proceeded to ask her something she wasn't expecting at all.

"Kat, I'd like you to come to Todos Santos to visit me there. It only seems fair that you see where I live, now that I have seen where you live. However, I must tell you that Carmen would never stand for you coming to stay in a single man's home without a chaperone. She'll insist that you bring some other woman with you. Do you have a friend you could bring and perhaps stay for several days to vacation?"

As Kat considered his offer, it dawned on her that her friend Barb would have time off between her summer school duties and when school started up again after Labor Day. "Yes, I do have a friend who could perhaps come with me!" she exclaimed. JD told her that they were welcome anytime. With that, Kat told him she'd check in with Barb and let him know. "Oh, how fun that would be. Will you let me ride one of your horses?" she asked.

"Of course you can, but you may have to ride with me first," he responded. Kat asked him if that's because he thought she didn't know how to ride a horse. He shot back with, "No, it's just that I'll use any excuse to put my arms around you, young lady."

As JD pulled into the parking lot that Kat had directed him to, she immediately pointed to her intended studio. They got out, and she took him for a short tour of the space. JD told her that he was happy she had found it and hoped that it would pay off as she imagined. He also asked her if he might commission her to create something for his villa. "Well, I'd love to do that after I see it and have a better sense of what would fit the home," she said. JD went on to tell Kat that she'd get a good sense of the art of his country when she came to visit as Todos Santos was a bit of an artist's haven. He could tell that Kat was intrigued by that prospect, and he hoped it might increase her resolve to come visit his home.

As the two made their way back to the car, Kat asked if he knew of the Old Fisherman's Grotto restaurant in Monterey. JD said he'd never been to Monterey until he landed at the airport this morning. Kat was excited to show him her little corner of the world, so she directed him to the place where they enjoyed dinner together.

During the meal, Kat hesitatingly inquired about how safe he was after the events that had taken place. Sensing her fears for him, and also wanting to make sure she felt safe traveling to his country, he assured her that the worst had passed, and she should not worry. "Well, while my brother will not be able to return to the university to complete his studies, the sleepy little town of Todos Santos is a very safe place."

After dinner, the two drove back to her cottage in Carmel, where JD reminded her that Carmen would be appalled that he had spent hours in her home alone with her. Kat told him that she'd try not to ever bring that up in conversation if she visited him at his villa. Rearing back and raising his voice a bit, he asked, "If?" Kat quickly revised her comments to "when." Satisfied with that, JD asked her if they might walk on the beach and watch the sunset before he had to leave. Kat was in no hurry to let him go, so she fished for her keys and then dropped her purse in the foyer, locking the door as they headed for the beach across the street.

Walking on the warm sand at dusk was one of Kat's favorite things to do, but it did require taking off her shoes. As she was slipping them off, JD held her hand to help with balance, all the while admiring her lovely form. In his mind, he had already placed her on his beach, wearing just her swimsuit. As she looked up at him, she caught him staring at her. He momentarily looked away, but his smile gave him away.

"Penny for your thoughts," said Kat.

JD looked puzzled and asked if that was an American quiz game of some sort. Once she explained the colloquialism, it was his turn to blush. "I'm not sure you really want to know what I was thinking at that moment," he said sheepishly. "In fact, I'm not sure I was thinking as much as I was imagining."

With that, he stopped walking and turned his body to face hers in order that he might kiss her with many kisses. The two were entwined for about a minute before he stopped and suggested that they'd better keep walking, or he'd never stop kissing her.

CHAPTER 19

When Kat woke up the next morning, she pulled the covers over her head. If only she could go back to sleep and dream about last night's walk on the beach before JD left her again. In that moment, she was conscious of the fact that she was pouting. Resolved to see him again, she got herself dressed for the day, and before long, she was on the phone to Barb to make plans to vacation in Sur Baja.

"Barbie, it's Kat, and have I got a deal for you! You. . . me. . . in Baja for four days on the beach, and I'm buying! What do you say?" Barb squealed, which Kat took as a good sign.

"I'd love to!" Barb responded. "Of course, I only have a two-week window at the end of this month before I have to begin prepping for the school year."

The two spent about an hour on the phone talking about Kat's new studio start-up, Barb's love of her new job, and more. But when it came time to discuss the details of the trip, Kat knew she'd have to let Barb in on her secret. She reminded Barb of her trip to Europe earlier in the summer and then began to reveal the details of meeting a tall, dark, handsome Mexican man from Baja. Barb was thoroughly engrossed until she put two and two together.

"Wait," she exclaimed, "are you telling me you're taking me on a trip to see this guy? What's in it for me? Does he have a brother or something?"

Kat laughed and told Barb, "Why, yes, actually he does; three to be exact!"

It took some work to convince Barb that she wouldn't be excess baggage during the whole trip and that she had a duty as a best friend to oversee the whole thing. Barb agreed to go to Todos Santos with the understanding that she had veto power over this relationship if she didn't think JD was right for Kat. Willing to go along with that arrangement, Kat was certain that Barb was going to find JD to be the gentleman she knew him to be.

Kat spent the rest of the morning handcrafting a card to send to JD to suggest possible dates when she and Barb could come for a short visit. The card was made of a deep red fiber paper, and Kat had created a beautiful paper quilled fish for the front. She'd have to place it in a special envelope so it didn't crush the artwork. Inside she wrote with white ink the following:

> *August 16, 1980*
>
> *Dear JD,*
>
> *Thank you for the brief but ever-so-sweet personal visit you made to Carmel this week. I remain saddened to hear of your pain and loss. However, I can't even begin to tell you how wonderful it was to hear from you again—and better still, to see you again.*
>
> *I have checked in with my friend, Barb Beasley, and we are able to come for a short visit sometime in the last week of August. I don't want to*

overstay our welcome, so could you please let me know what your best four days are within that timeframe? Once I know what works best for you I will make our flight arrangements from Los Angeles to La Paz.

Your friend,

Katarina

CHAPTER 20

As Kat pulled into the church parking lot on Sunday morning, she was running so late that she failed to notice the car she parked next to was Jason's. As she grabbed her purse and hurriedly made her way to the front doors, she saw his large frame leaning up against a post in the breezeway. For a split second, she felt like telling him all about her visitor of last week but dismissed the thought as Jason greeted her with a hug while asking her if her alarm clock failed to go off this morning. Kat felt the need to explain her tardiness, but the two instead slipped into a back pew to the quiet hush of silent prayer.

After the service, Kat had her opportunity to thank Jason for making the drive to see her. He seemed genuinely eager to spend as much of the day with her as he could, so they headed off to Seaside for lunch. It was over this meal that Kat sensed that perhaps things were getting more serious when Jason piped up with a question.

"So, Kat, what's the job market in Carmel like?" he inquired.

"It's such a small village, Jason. And unless one feels like pumping gas, slinging hash, or trying to sell artwork, there's really not much work available. Why do you ask?" prompted Kat.

"Oh, I don't know; it's just that this job of mine is so stressful. It's not that the work is difficult, though I live in constant fear of messing up because my boss is such a bully. And that causes everyone in the department to be in competition with each other in hopes that they can be the one to avoid his public ridicule."

"That sounds positively dreadful," remarked Kat as she dragged the bill from Jason's side of the table over to herself.

"Hey, maybe I could work with you in that shop you are starting up! I could do everything from marketing to handyman work around the place," exclaimed Jason. No sooner had he blurted that out than he realized how unrealistic it sounded. "I guess that sounded crazy, but I hope you know it's only because I want to spend more time with you."

Leaning across the table, Kat started in with "I enjoy spending time with you, Jason. However, I feel like I need to tell you something about a trip I took earlier this summer."

Jason interrupted, "Hey, let's drive up to Monterey, and you can tell me all about your vacation!"

"What's up in Monterey that has your attention this afternoon?" asked Kat.

Jason told her that he needed to find some new work clothes, and he wanted her opinion on what to get. "Sure, that sounds like fun, but we'd better drive separately so you can get home more quickly from there," responded Kat with her usual logic. The two agreed upon the department store where they'd meet to take care of this little chore.

After wandering through the men's department of the store, Jason settled on a couple of dress shirts, a tie, a pair of slacks, and a blazer. As he was finishing up in the dressing room after trying on several items, Kat was at the checkout handing the salesman her credit card and telling him she'd pay for everything. Just as Jason made his way to the desk, Kat turned to hand him the receipt with a smile saying, "Now, you're in no position to be paying for all this, but you'll need the receipt in case something doesn't work out and needs to be returned. Got it?"

"Are you kidding? You're buying all this for me?" asked Jason with eyes wide in surprise. Jason then leaned over to plant a big kiss on her cheek as Kat went on to insist that he consider them a gift since she knew she'd missed his birthday last March.

"Well, thank you, Kat! That wasn't necessary, but you're a gem for helping out this struggling junior lender! And hey, at least I'll look good when my boss is chewing me out!"

As the two reached their cars to go their separate ways, Jason once again pulled Kat to himself and told her how glad he was that they were seeing each other again. As he was explaining that he'd call her during the week, Kat interrupted to tell him that she and Barb were going to Mexico for a few days.

"Oh, yeah? Another vacation so soon? You're quite the jetsetter, aren't you? Well, when you get back, you'll have to tell me how you spent your summer vacations. Meanwhile, I'll be struggling along in Sacramento just trying to make a few bucks!" joked Jason.

As she drove home that early evening, Kat felt guilty about not telling Jason the whole story about her upcoming trip. Then again, she thought, she'd be sure to bring it up when he called her later in the week.

CHAPTER 21

Despite the sun now setting over the horizon, the heat in Todos Santos was taking its toll on the horses as well as Bernardo. Taking the bandana from his back pocket, he wiped the sweat from his face before watering the horses once more before dinner. He knew it would end up making him late for the meal and that Carmen would get after him for it once he made his way to the kitchen in the main house. As he finished up and made his way to the back door entry, he didn't even see Carmen. However, he did see the table set for the two of them off in the corner of the kitchen.

As he was preparing to wash his hands in the large stainless steel sink, he could hear Carmen laughing and talking with JD in the hallway. No sooner had he finished up than he saw the two of them walking into the kitchen. It wasn't often Bernardo saw JD in the kitchen as it was Carmen's domain and she didn't usually want her employer there. However, this evening seemed a bit different as JD was following her while attempting to retrieve something she had in her hand. The two were carrying on in the native tongue when Bernardo asked what was going on. Carmen told Bernardo that JD's lady friend had sent him a pretty card saying she was coming for a visit and bringing her best friend.

JD finally retrieved the card from Carmen's hand and winked at her as he announced that everyone must be on their best behavior when Katarina arrived. Bernardo had heard a bit about this woman JD had met in Paris, but it wasn't until now that he realized just how smitten JD really was. Chiding him a bit, Bernardo remarked that JD would be good for nothing the entire time this woman was here—and just when there were young horses to be broken.

JD translated the card while Carmen and Bernardo continued to tease their boss. In truth, both the housekeeper and the caretaker had often had conversations in the past about how wonderful it would be for JD to find a good woman and settle down. As JD finished reading, Carmen heard the word *amiga* and immediately shook her head from side to side and clucked her tongue. JD could see her disappointment and reached over to give her a big hug, assuring her that he'd do his best to make Kat more than a friend during this upcoming visit. Carmen pushed JD away with her hand, even as she blushed and turned away smiling.

After having dinner with his brother in the dining room, JD retired to the large dark wood desk in his office. Picking up the red card from his desk, he admired the paper art on the front again. Rereading Kat's words, he then flipped the card onto the desk, and it landed with the back page facing him. His eye caught a small inscription on the bottom right-hand corner of the card, a beautiful swirl of entwined letters in black ink—KS. Of course, he thought to himself, she made this with her own hand. He was momentarily ashamed for having forgotten that Kat was as talented as she was sweet. He would send his response via telegram first thing in the morning, asking her to plan the visit during the last week in August...and to be sure to bring her swimsuit.

CHAPTER 22

Kat was thrilled to receive JD's telegram pleading with her to come to Todos Santos for the last four days in August as it seemed to fit best with his business schedule.

Making contact with Barb, who was also very excited about heading down to Sur Baja on August 28, Kat arranged to drive down to stay with Barb the night before so they could head to the airport early the next morning. With their tickets purchased, it was now just a matter of counting the days!

Kat was keeping busy with getting the studio into shape and contacting local artists about consignment. She was also putting out feelers for potential students, as well as figuring out how much she might charge nonstudents for use of the pottery making equipment. She had already brought in a local Seaside outfit to do some basics around patching and painting walls, replacing flooring, and even repositioning lighting for the best angles on artwork in the front of the shop. Finally, Kat had placed an order for the exterior signage that needed to comply with city and landlord regulations. It was all fun, but it was also keeping her from calling Jason, despite the message he had left on her answering machine wishing her and Barb a safe trip to Mexico and urging her to call him when she got back.

On the morning of August 27, Kat finally finished packing the last items into her suitcase and locked up the cottage. She had stopped the mail, let Larry know she was leaving the country again, and made sure her neighbor knew to keep an eye on things. Piling things into the car, she began the long trip to Pasadena to be with Barb and her parents this evening.

The drive was fairly uneventful, and Kat only stopped once for some lunch. One of Kat's least favorite things in life was eating alone, so she had brought her Spanish language book from high school days with her. Trying to brush up on her vocabulary and verb tenses seemed like the thing to do if she was going to be meeting JD's family, friends, employees, or anyone else in his sphere. She figured it might also be a help to Barb who had taken German while in college, in addition to sign language classes. Kat smiled to herself as she thought of her friend knowing more German than she did.

Kat pulled into the Beasley's driveway about 3:00 p.m. just as Barb was making her way out to the streetside mailbox. It was perfect timing for the two friends to hug and then rush inside the air-conditioned house on this hot day. It was just the two friends together that afternoon, at least until Barb's parents got home from their respective jobs. Barb wanted Kat to help her prepare a nice dinner for everyone this evening, so they started planning and ended up at the grocery store where Kat insisted on buying the ingredients for their feast.

The two friends always seemed to simply pick up where they left off because they were just that comfortable together. They talked while preparing the evening meal, which wasn't perfect but seemed to be good enough. The family especially enjoyed the dessert, probably because Kat and Barb had not exactly slaved over the store-bought ice cream!

After dinner, the two friends parked in front of the TV to watch a movie together. As they were waiting for the show to start, Kat mentioned to Barb that she'd reconnected with Jason Gabriel recently. Barb's reaction wasn't what Kat was expecting.

"What? Are you kidding me? You're dating Jason again, but we're going to Sur Baja so you can see another man? Does Jason know about him? Does this JD fellow know about Jason?"

Kat just smiled and said, "Too many questions, Barb. Jason and I are just getting reacquainted, and I did tell him I was taking a trip to Sur Baja with you."

Barb shot back with, "You didn't tell him about JD, did you, Kat?"

"Oh, Barbie, I don't know that I owe Jason an explanation. I'm single, remember? Besides, I don't really know that anything will come of either one of these relationships," responded Kat.

Barb seemed only minimally satisfied with that answer, mumbling as the movie was starting, "You should have told Jason why you were going."

The next morning Barb and Kat were filled with the excitement of travel, seeing a new part of the world and wondering what they might encounter. After breakfast and goodbyes to Mr. and Mrs. Beasley, the two were headed to LAX to make their flight to La Paz. They would arrive around lunchtime, and Kat had assurances from JD that he'd be there to collect them at the airport.

In fact, as they were winging their way to La Paz, Kat was remembering the phone call with JD a few nights earlier. It was one of those late night calls where they almost spoke in whispers, even though no one else was around. JD had told Kat about his long day at work and how exhausted he was, but that hearing her voice revived him. And Kat drifted off to sleep that night reveling in the sound of his voice in her head. She could hardly wait to hear that voice again.

CHAPTER 23

Sitting by the window, Barb pointed out what looked like an airport, and Kat leaned over her to look. Kat could see the surrounding reddish-beige dirt spreading out from the light grey landing strip. The landscape was definitely flat, though not terribly unlike Southern California she thought. As the plane descended, the palm trees and cactus surrounding the small terminal building were coming into view. Within moments, they landed safely, and the pilot was speaking Spanish overhead. Barb looked over at Kat with that "What's he saying?" look on her face, so Kat just whispered, "Welcome to La Paz, where the time is now 12:05 p.m."

There was no doubt that Barb was excited about being in Sur Baja, but Kat's heart was racing for the thought of seeing JD. As they gathered their things in preparation for disembarking, Barb grabbed Kat's arm, looked her straight in the eye, and said, "Spare me the kissing stuff, okay?"

Kat laughed so hard she thought she'd cry! "Really, Barb, you are so silly. Besides, I don't want him to spare me the kissing stuff!"

As the two exited the plane into the blazing sun and heat of the day, they were beginning to wonder how wise it was to visit this part of the world in late August. However, they were both looking forward to this adventure of theirs. Kat's eyes were scanning the building, but there were few large windows. She figured they'd have to get inside to see JD. Just steps inside, the two found themselves in a somewhat air-conditioned holding room where they were directed to a long line for checking passports and some questioning. Once they were cleared, they were able to pick up their luggage that had been lined up against a wall in the room. Kat's patience in getting through all of this was wearing thin.

Once they walked through the solid doors of the holding room, they could see the length of the small airport, and Kat was getting concerned as she scanned the faces of those nearby but didn't see JD. With Barb following right behind her, there in the distance she could see JD walking toward them. The moment of recognition almost made Kat weak in the knees for she wondered if the man might just be getting better looking every time she saw him. As he approached the ladies, he was smiling broadly, and Barb caught on quickly that this must be Kat's JD. He leaned toward Kat to kiss her on the cheek and promptly put out his hand to shake Barb's hand saying, "You must be Barb."

Barb was having one of those rare speechless moments as he also leaned over to kiss her on the cheek. "Uh, yeah... Barb... Kat's friend."

JD then reached down to pick up their suitcases, saying, "Follow me beautiful ladies, and welcome to my home."

The two did as they were instructed and answered JD's many questions as he walked them to his shiny red truck back out in the hot sun. Yes, the flight was fine, and yes, it surely was hotter here than back home, they responded. JD explained that La Paz was often about 10 degrees hotter than where his ranch was located, so he appreciated getting out of town after already having been at his business for several hours this morning. Kat asked him if he'd have to return to La Paz to work during their visit, but JD assured his guests that they would have his full attention while visiting Todos Santos.

With Barb insisting on sitting in the backseat, Kat sat in the front passenger seat next to JD. As he was pulling out of the parking spot, she commented on how she wasn't expecting him to be driving a Ford Bronco. "Well, it's only because I couldn't afford a Ford burro!" JD joked. The three got a good laugh over that one, though Kat wasn't sure if she'd stepped in it with her comment. However, JD reached over to pat her hand as if to reassure her. She was reassured, at least until she observed JD remove a handgun from his belt under his loose-fitting white shirt and place it in the center console storage. She looked over at him, but he had his eyes fixed on the road ahead as they pulled out onto a main thoroughfare.

"So are you ladies as hungry as I am?" inquired JD. The two were absolutely ready for lunch and couldn't wait to have some authentic Mexican food. With that, JD announced that he'd take them to one of his favorite eateries— La Perla. He mentioned that he knew the owner, who JD speculated might treat him with more respect if he walked in with two beautiful women. Kat could hear Barb snicker in the backseat over that one, so she turned to give her a stern look just as Barb put on her innocent face and turned to stare out the window.

Now filled with great food and having had a wonderful time getting to know each other while at the restaurant in La Paz, the three were making their way to JD's ranch when he began to explain what the ladies might expect as a daily routine at his place. He mentioned that they'd arrive just before 3:00 p.m., and he would turn them over to Carmen, who would see that they were comfortably established in their respective rooms.

Barb interjected at that point asking him, "Does that mean we both have own room?" JD responded affirmatively but added that he wasn't sure which bedrooms Carmen had selected for them. With that, Barb's eyes got wider, and she dared asked, "Just how many rooms does your ranch have?"

JD just smiled and said, "We'll count them when we get there."

After the long drive, they pulled off the main road to a smaller dirt road; Kat asked JD if they were getting closer to his ranch. He indicated that indeed they were and were turning west toward the water now, though the town of Todos Santos was off the road they had just left. Barb piped up that it seemed this part of the landscape was a bit less desert-like and had more vegetation. JD explained that Todos Santos had a natural underground spring that fed the area, which meant it was an excellent location for crops. He went on to tell them that it had once been known for sugar cane and other agricultural business but that there was a bit less of that now. He said that the town was small, just a few thousand residents, but growing. He also mentioned that it had recently attracted several artists, Americans, and others who wanted the slower lifestyle that Baja offered.

As they made their way toward what looked like an endless horizon, Kat noticed some cows ahead on the road. JD slowed down as they approached. The cattle seemed in no hurry to move along on this hot summer day. But once they were clear of the roadway, JD continued on toward the blue horizon.

"Are we close to the ocean now?" she asked.

JD pointed to a turn in the road ahead and explained that they would parallel the ocean toward the ranch. That turn was onto a simple dirt road, one even a bit bumpier than before. However, the passengers were having a wonderful time looking at the scenery and spotting the ranch ahead. They noticed the cactus and slight vegetation in the increasingly sandy soil. Soon they were driving past a long barn next to a large, fenced horse corral. Outside of the barn stood an older man who took his hat off and waved it as they drove by. JD waved back and let the two women know, "That's Bernardo, and you'll meet him later this afternoon."

As they approached the sprawling villa on the beach, they passed through a large, beautiful wrought iron gate and onto the ranch. The visitors were in awe as they passed the whitewashed stucco mission-style home, with its beautiful ironwork lamp sconces beside each of the huge hand-carved wooden front double doors. As JD pulled into the circular driveway, he parked near what appeared to be a small courtyard with an entry behind a lovely stone fountain. The grounds were beautiful, despite the season. Kat couldn't help but mention how much it seemed like an oasis in a cactus desert. JD told her she would be amazed how much more lush the plant life was during the other seasons.

As the three got out of the truck, JD took their bags from the back of the vehicle and escorted the two women through the courtyard that was lined with hanging vines and colorful pots filled with plants. The courtyard walkway was made of large terra-cotta tiles that matched the tile roof. Kat was taking it all in when a short, stocky older woman emerged from the doorway. Her face was weathered, but her smile was broad. Kat knew immediately that it must be Carmen. JD began speaking rapidly in Spanish to the woman as Carmen backed into the house to let the three come through the doorway. He put the bags down and turned to Kat and Barb and introduced them to Carmen who had a precious way about her as she spoke in her native language; some of which Kat could understand. To Kat, the most fun was to hear Carmen say all the r's in "Katarina y Barbara" with that accent!

JD explained that he would follow Carmen to their rooms where he would drop off their bags. He then mentioned that the ladies could then rest and relax from their trip.

"Rest?" asked Barb in surprise.

JD scratched his forehead as he realized the two might not be familiar with the afternoon siesta concept, so he proceeded to tell them that they might want to take advantage of their siesta because in his household the second half of the day was from about 5:00 p.m. to midnight. He reminded them that they wouldn't even see dinner on the table until 8:00 p.m. at the earliest.

Kat looked at Barb and said, "I think I could get used to that kind of schedule!"

Finally tucked away in their bedrooms that were joined by a large common bathroom, the two ladies thanked Carmen and their host profusely. JD agreed to meet them back in the small courtyard around 5:30 p.m. for refreshments before he gave them the grand tour of the ranch. He lingered a bit too long at Kat's door in hopes of stealing a kiss, but Carmen was already shooing him back down the hall.

Once they were in their rooms, Kat and Barb immediately met in the bathroom to decide which room was the best for a bit of chatting and giggling. They were like school girls as they landed on Kat's big four-poster mahogany bed where she let out a big sigh.

"Isn't he dreamy, Barb?" she asked.

Barb rolled her eyes saying, "Beyond dreamy, Kat, he's drop-dead gorgeous! You were right, and I just want you to know that I already approve. He's quite the gentleman too. Now, what did you say his brother's name is?"

CHAPTER 24

Kat and Barb did finally snooze a bit in their rooms but started dashing around to make themselves look presentable at about 5:15 p.m. so that they could meet JD in the courtyard. Eager to see more of the ranch, the ladies were heading down the hallway hoping they could find their way back to the place they had entered the magnificent villa. As they retraced their steps, they admired the beautiful tile floors, rugs, hanging black iron lamps, and artwork along the way. As they did, Kat remembered that JD had commissioned her to produce an art piece that he could put in the home. As she looked around, she felt pretty inadequate to the task, given some of the beautiful and large art pieces he already had on display in his home.

As they exited the door to the courtyard, the heat was all too apparent again. However, JD stood up from his seat in a corner of the covered portion of the patio and was beckoning them to come over and join him. There were two wicker loveseats and a few chairs clustered in the shade surrounding a low table upon which sat a tray with two pitchers and some glass tumblers. Kat noticed that JD had pulled his hair back in a ponytail and had changed his shirt to something slightly more formal in a light blue color. As the ladies sat down, he asked them if they preferred lemonade or sangria. Both of them decided to stick with lemonade on this very warm evening.

Kat wasn't quite sure why she felt a bit nervous as she looked over at JD, who appeared to be so relaxed. She thought perhaps it was because she wanted so much to hold his attention, but in a way that didn't make Barb feel awkward. While the three sipped on their drinks, JD's brother Antonio stepped out of the house to join them. JD was quick to introduce him to the ladies, and Antonio promptly kissed the hands of both Barb and Kat. His English was limited, but he was able to express his greetings and welcome them to Sur Baja. As he poured himself some sangria, JD suggested that it might be time to give the ladies a tour of the villa and the stables before making their way down to the beach for sunset. Kat and Barb were definitely up for that and said so with their eager faces.

JD and Antonio stood to escort the ladies, explaining that this small patio was an area where they enjoyed spending evenings, though the much larger courtyard on the other side of the villa faced the ocean. JD directed the ladies back inside, and as they stood in the entry, he explained that the home was constructed in a squared off U-shape which surrounded the large courtyard that looked out toward the beach. They were on the north leg which contained a large kitchen, a pantry, and the laundry area on one side, and the dining area and his office on the courtyard side.

As they passed through these areas, Kat continued to admire the artwork, lighting, mirrors, glass, tiles, and more. Barb, on the other hand, was continually impressed with the size of the place and finally asked JD about the square footage. As they entered his office, he indicated the home

was about 6,000 square feet. As they were taking in the
masculine dark furniture in the room, Kat spotted the red
paper quilled card she had sent was propped up on the
desk. JD had hardly been able to take his eyes off of Kat, and
this time he followed her eyes as she saw the card. Walking
to her side, he told her that her handiwork was amazing.
Blushing, she thanked him for saying so.

As they continued the tour by walking through the dining room and the office, they couldn't help but notice the
floor-to-ceiling windows. Through those windows, one
could easily see the expansive courtyard of white stone tiles
that seemed to fade off into the tan sands of the beach. As
the four returned to the starting point of the tour, Antonio
excused himself to head back out to the patio to fill his glass
again. The three then proceeded back toward the hallway
of bedrooms. But instead of turning the corner, they continued straight ahead through a large arched doorway that
opened up into an expansive living room with many seating
areas, a huge fireplace, large paintings, and even a black
grand piano. At the front of the living room were the mas-
sive carved dark wood front doors that they saw when they
drove up to the villa. And at the back of the living room
was a doorway to a large theater-style room. JD took them
through that door, and after they admired the entertainment room, he brought them out another door that put
them at the other end of the hall of bedrooms. They could
see their bedrooms on one side, and two other bedrooms
and a bathroom across the hall from theirs. Apparently, Carmen stayed in the bedroom closest to the kitchen but had a
lovely view of the courtyard from her room. As they moved
over to the southern leg of the home, they encountered one
very large bathroom, and the remaining part of this leg of
the home was the master suite. Apparently, this was JD's

retreat, and he did not open the double door entry for the ladies to see inside.

Barb had been counting and blurted out, "Five bedrooms and three bathrooms?"

JD laughed and then corrected her with, "Actually four bedrooms, three bathrooms, and a complete master suite."

Barb cocked her head to one side and asked, "If Carmen lives here and your brother is here, where does Bernardo stay?"

JD told Barb that was a perfect segue as Bernardo actually had living quarters in the stable that they were about to visit.

Now it was Kat's turn to get excited. "Oh, does that mean we get to see the horses?"

Once again, JD smiled and said, "Well, it will be hard to miss them!"

The trio made their way back to the small courtyard where they caught Antonio playing some lovely acoustic guitar music, with his feet up on the chair across from him. As he finished the number, the women were going on about how talented he was. Antonio seemed to understand that they liked the music and smiled as he put the guitar down so he could rejoin the tour.

JD decided to lead the group up to the stable via the circular drive so they could pass by the beautiful sixteen-foot front double doors of the home. Kat stopped there for a few moments to trace the woodwork with her finger, while JD explained that his father, Eduardo, had been intimately involved in the creation of the doors when he renovated the home after inheriting the ranch from his great-grandfather. The whole conversation reminded Kat that the two sons of Eduardo were still in mourning, and it seemed to show on their faces.

As they hiked along a dusty walking trail to the stable, they could see Bernardo working with one of the horses inside the corral. Antonio walked ahead to tell Bernardo something over the fence in Spanish, while JD directed Kat and Barb into the stable, which contained a dozen stalls. As they walked down the center of the stable, Kat could see lovely horses in all but two stalls. At the back of the stable was a door that JD pointed to and explained that was the living quarters for Bernardo.

Barb was petting the face of one of the horses when she asked JD, "Which one of your horses is your favorite?"

JD explained, "Most of the horses you see here are boarders, and some are new trainees that I will eventually sell. However, Barb, I believe you have picked out the best horse in the bunch—my horse!"

Kat jumped in to inquire, "Does your horse have a name?"

JD proceeded to pull back an old blanket that had been thrown over the stall door, revealing a small wooden sign with the name El Jefe.

With a big grin on her face, Kat countered with, "Wait a minute. I thought you were 'The Boss'!"

JD just smiled and said, "I guess I have more respect for the horse than the horse has for me, hence the name!"

As the three emerged from the stable, they encountered Antonio with Bernardo. JD introduced the older, dark-skinned man to the two women, and he shook hands with both. Bernardo seemed to be skilled with horses but a bit awkward and shy around the ladies. Kat chalked it up to the fact that Bernardo also did not speak much English. Pointing to the horse still remaining in the corral, JD spoke with Bernardo in Spanish for several minutes before it was time to depart for the beach.

Walking through a sandy trail that was lined with clumps of tall yellow and green grass, the four young adults finally ended up on the beach as the sun was beginning to set. Kat and JD had now paired off, leaving Antonio to struggle through his limited English with Barb. However, as Kat looked back at the two walking along the beach together, she noted that they didn't seem to be having much difficulty communicating. Kat was just glad to have JD to herself for a moment, especially as he reached for her hand and reminded her of the sunset they had shared in Carmel earlier in the month.

"So which sunset is more beautiful, yours or mine?" he asked her.

Kat looked over at her handsome host and answered, "All the ones we share." JD moved closer to put his arm around her, and Kat thrilled to be close to him.

Before long, Antonio and Barb had caught up to the slower moving Kat and JD. Barb called out to JD asking him about a small building on the beach off in the distance.

"Who lives there?" she inquired.

Kat had been so engrossed in JD she hadn't even noticed the cabin-like structure that was set back about 400 feet from the high-water tidemark. As the four walked together now, JD explained that what they saw ahead was a place he had built himself a few years earlier.

As they approached the cabin, he pulled keys from his pocket and unlocked the door to reveal a cozy one-room space that contained a beautiful bed with white canopy netting, an antique dresser with attached mirror, a rocking chair, and an old trunk at the foot of the bed. It was small, rustic, and perfectly dressed for a beach house.

In her typical forthright style, Barb announced, "But it has no bathroom."

JD looked over at Barb and said, "You have discovered my design flaw, Barb. You should have been an architect!" Barb blushed, yet even as the four were leaving the cabin, she was still insisting that it needed a bathroom.

Making their way back along the beach to the main house, they took a left that would eventually lead them right to the large courtyard that was now lit up with outdoor lighting. Carmen could be seen setting a table that was located nearest the house, just past an outdoor patio seating area. As they arrived at the courtyard and stepped onto the tiles, Kat asked JD if they would be dining outside tonight. He confirmed that dinner would be served on the courtyard and that they should all take time to wash up for the meal and meet back at the table within five to ten minutes.

As Barb and Kat headed back to their bedrooms and bathroom, they were chattering away about the beauty and expanse of the villa. Barb was hoping they could spend time on the beach tomorrow, and Kat was looking forward to riding a horse. The two took turns in the bathroom and within their allotted time were making their way back to the courtyard to join the brothers there.

CHAPTER 25

The dinner that Carmen had put before them was absolutely delightful, and JD made sure she heard about it each time she came out to check on the foursome. Their conversation was wide ranging. JD had opened the meal with a wonderful prayer, and then there were language lessons, some funny stories, some family history, discussions about the trauma the young men had gone through recently, talk about the future, and even a recounting of how JD had met Kat. It also seemed that Barb and Antonio had hit it off, even though the two struggled to understand each other. Thankfully, JD was a willing interpreter through it all.

As they finished the meal under the indigo sky filled with stars and a nearly full moon, it was nearing 10:00 p.m. Barb was the first to yawn, and soon she was excusing herself for bed. That prompted Antonio to retire to the kitchen to help Carmen with clean-up. JD and Kat were finally alone, so they decided to walk along the beach on this lovely summer night. Still about 78 degrees, they welcomed the slight breeze off the ocean as they talked lowly and walked slowly.

"I didn't think things could get more romantic than Paris, JD," said Kat. "But here we are on a beach in Baja on a beautiful evening, and I think it may top Paris." JD seemed to agree as he put his arms around her waist and looked into her moonlit eyes. Without a word, his eyes seemed to be pleading with her, yet she wasn't sure what to say.

After several seconds passed, he spoke. "Kat, do you love me?"

Now frozen in place, Kat was even less certain of what to say. Mustering up her strongest voice, she responded, "Why, I've never had a man ask me such a bold question."

JD squeezed her shoulders with his hands and said, "Perhaps that's because no man has ever wanted to hear you say yes as much as I do. For you see, Kat, I am certain that I love you—and only wait to hear that you feel the same way."

Rather than awaiting her response, JD immediately and passionately kissed her. Once again, Kat felt as though her knees would give way as the two reveled in the kiss that lasted so long. Perhaps JD sensed her weakness because he picked her up to carry her back toward the villa. With her arms around his neck, Kat revealed, "JD, I've never been in love before, and yet my feelings for you are overwhelming. But, is this love, or is it infatuation?"

JD released her to stand on her own and then taking her hands in his, he asked her to consider her feelings for him and answer his question only when she was ready. He then held her close and kissed her again, and Kat was once again lost in him.

CHAPTER 26

The morning sun came streaming into Kat's bedroom through the large skylight above her bed, causing her to open her eyes. Right away, she felt the flood of emotion that JD had placed in her heart the night before when he asked her if she loved him. As she lay there in the bed trying to assess her true feelings for him, she noticed Barb slowly opening her door to the common bathroom to see if Kat was awake. Kat tried closing her eyes quickly, but Barb had already caught her awake!

"Get up, you lazy bones!" said Barb as she busted into Kat's bedroom. "How was the rest of your evening? Did you get some time alone with your Latin dreamboat?"

Kat sat up in bed, pulled her knees to her chest, and smiled. "Why, yes I did," she explained. "In fact, we walked on the beach by the moonlight. It was so romantic."

With that, Barb injected, "Well, you promised me three brothers, but two of them, we now know, are married with kids, and I'm not altogether sure that Antonio is my type." Kat resisted the urge to apologize and instead changed the subject to the matter of finding some breakfast this morning.

After getting showered and dressed, the two were making their way down the hall toward the kitchen when Barb asked Kat if she was going to tell Jason about JD, or at least tell JD about Jason. Just as Barb finished her sentence, the two of them could hear footsteps behind them. As they turned around, they saw JD turning the corner to catch up with them.

"Good morning, ladies! It's time for some good strong coffee to prepare us for a day of play!" exclaimed JD. The ladies were intrigued as they let JD lead the way toward the dining room.

"What will we be playing?" asked Barb, to which JD responded that he thought it might be a great day to ride horses, spend time on the beach, and perhaps head into town later to have dinner at a small cantina he liked. He also mentioned that Antonio would be joining them, though he would be leaving the next morning for Los Cabos where he'd be taking up residence now that he'd taken a job working there with their oldest brother César.

As the three entered the dining room, they were greeted by Antonio who stood up to help seat Barb, while JD assisted Kat. The table settings for all four were already in place, as was the full coffee pot. Carmen had provided a platter of fruit, cheese, nuts, and rolls with butter and jam. As Kat was eyeing the breakfast with anticipation, she looked over to see JD's head bowed in silent prayer. She thought she'd better follow suit, and so did Barb.

At the end of the table was a Spanish language newspaper, and after the prayer, Antonio got up to retrieve it and hand it to JD, while saying something to JD in Spanish. JD apparently felt the need to interpret for his guests, so he excused himself for a moment to read the front page of the paper from La Paz that Antonio handed him. After quietly reading for a few minutes, he frowned a bit and let Kat and Barb know that he felt the government officials were determined to stand in the way of progress in the region. Neither one of the ladies wanted to probe much further on that matter as they watched JD drop the paper in disgust onto the empty chair next to him.

With that, JD announced that there would be riding lessons that morning and that the ladies seemed to be appropriately dressed in long pants but would need something a bit more substantial than their sandals. The two indicated that they had brought some walking shoes and they'd meet up at the small courtyard after they changed into those. Both Kat and Barb then made a move to gather up their plates to take them to the kitchen, but JD put his hand out to stop them. "If you do that, Carmen will think you're after her job!" he said.

CHAPTER 27

JD was apparently serious when he told Kat that she'd first have to ride with him. Antonio had helped Barb onto the smoky black El Jefe, before leading the horse into the corral. But JD helped Kat mount a young horse that was new to the stable, and then he climbed on to sit behind her in the large western saddle. He took the reins, and with his arms around Kat, he told her to hang onto the saddle horn with both hands. The horse seemed a bit skittish as they exited the stable, yet it settled into a slow walk as JD moved toward the corral. As he did, he explained to Kat that he was still working with this horse to teach it his leads. Kat didn't know what that meant, but she was excited to learn more... and to be close to JD. He leaned over to kiss her sleeveless exposed shoulder, which caused her to literally shiver, even on this hot day. He felt it and proceeded to say, "I can only hope that I always have that effect on you."

The day seemed to fly by between the horseback riding, the chatter in the stable, a brief tractor ride, and lunch. It was JD who eagerly prompted Kat and Barb to prepare for some time down at the beach after they had finished lunch. He promised to join them there after he took a phone call he was expecting.

117

As the two headed back to their rooms to get ready for the beach, in a hushed tone, Kat told Barb that JD had specifically mentioned bringing her swimsuit in his invitation. Barb remarked she wasn't at all surprised that her handsome horseman would want to see her wearing a bit less. Kat smiled but was already feeling self-conscious at the thought. Barb just laughed and told Kat, "You'll give him something to think about when you get back home!" Kat wanted to tell her best friend what JD had asked her last night, but clearly, this discussion was not headed in that direction.

Barb and Kat were on the sandy trail heading down to the beach when they saw Antonio riding across the wet sand line of the tide. He waved and continued on his way. They spotted a couple of canvas sling-back beach chairs on the beach and figured Antonio must have deposited them there. Carmen had provided them each with a large beach towel which they dropped on the chairs.

The two had worn short cover-ups as they were getting concerned about all the sun exposure from the morning's adventure. However, they weren't on the beach but 10 minutes before they were too hot to leave them on. Deciding to get into the water to cool off, Barb unzipped her cover-up and took off for the surf. Kat had to pull hers over her head, and while it was inside out and still draped on her arms, she could see JD coming down the sandy path clapping. She could feel the flush of rising embarrassment on her cheeks.

Fighting off all of her natural tendencies toward modesty, she dropped the shirt onto the chair and ran for the water where Barb was already waist deep. As Kat looked back, she could see JD breaking into a run as he followed her into the water. Catching her as she strained to move against the waves, she had only made it to water levels just under the top of her two-piece pink gingham swimsuit when JD grabbed her arm and pulled her to himself. Barb was starting to swim away while yelling, "Oh no, the kissing shark!" With that, JD did kiss Kat, and they both reveled in feeling the warmth of each other's skin. As JD kissed her, she found herself dropping her arms down to feel the soft, dark hair on his chest with her fingertips.

Once JD had his kiss, he dove into the water head first and then reappeared several feet away from Barb, leaping out of the water to her shrieks.

"Did you really just call me a 'kissing shark'?" he asked.

Instead of answering, Barb just shoved water at him, and soon they were in a splashing fight. Kat watched from a distance, not wanting to get in the middle of all that. Barb was the California girl who loved the water, but Kat had always been more of a stay-on-the-beach type. She knew the mechanics of swimming but never felt all that comfortable in the water. As she stood by clutching her own arms, JD broke away to return to her.

"You look like you might need more holding, Kat," he said. All she could think of was just how right he was.

"Yes, please," she responded. All he could think of was just how much he wished he could hold her forever.

With the sun beating down on them for nearly an hour, it was decided that the two fair ladies should probably get back indoors for siesta time. JD folded up the chairs and carried them as he walked Kat and Barb back to the house. As they entered the door, Kat could literally feel the heat on her skin and thought perhaps a nap might come only after applying some cream she had seen on the dresser of her room. Parting to go their own ways, the household settled into a period of rest until about 5:00 p.m. As she was drifting off to sleep, Kat hoped she would see JD in her dreams just as she had last seen him—shirtless.

CHAPTER 28

That evening involved a grand trip into Todos Santos where the young people enjoyed a wonderful dinner, local guitar music, and the colorful surroundings of the town square. Kat got a real sense of some of the local art in the shop windows and was even introduced to a couple of artists who lived there. It made her think that perhaps she could take on the design and production of something she'd make for JD's home.

The next day brought hot but stormy weather, with thundershowers and humidity that kept the three indoors most of the day. They felt bad that Antonio had picked this for his moving day, but they spent the day watching movies in the home theater room and even playing some card games over lunch. Dinner was lovely as Carmen had taken the previous night off and was rested and eager to put on a feast for which she was praised profusely.

It had been difficult for JD to get Kat alone, so he was pleased that the night sky had cleared so they could get in one more walk on the beach. As they did, he held her hand and told her how beautiful she looked in her swimsuit the day before. Kat was glad JD couldn't see her blushing as she thanked him for the compliment. And he didn't stop there. He went on to tell her that it wasn't just her beautiful curves, eyes, hair, and face that he appreciated. He wanted Kat to know that what he felt for her went beyond the superficial. "Though your beauty goes on and on," JD explained, "it's you—the person you are—that I have fallen for, Kat. It seems your gentle ways draw people of all kinds to you. I know I am drawn to you, like a moth to a flame. So much so that I'm tempted to let you consume me with your fire."

As they continued their walk, Kat began to explain to JD that he was unlike any man she'd ever met before.

"Did you feel that way when you first met Jason?" JD inquired.

Kat was simultaneously stunned and embarrassed by his question as he went on. "I heard Barb mention his name. Is there something you aren't telling me, Kat?" She now felt terrible for not having said something to both men.

Pouring out the events of the many weeks in which she had heard nothing from him, she explained that Jason had reentered her life and appeared to be interested in picking up where they left off when they were in college. As the explanation proceeded, JD never once looked away from her, making things even more difficult for her. When the whole story was out, he once again reminded her that he would not pressure her on the earlier question of her feelings for him.

But Kat returned to her earlier comments by reminding him that he had stirred something in her that she'd never felt before. She told him that she admired and respected him greatly for his upright character and his willingness to take responsibility on so many levels.

"I am in awe of how many people you take care of, JD," said Kat. "In fact, I feel a bit guilty that you've had to be responsible for Barb and me these past days, when you have a farm, a business, your family, and your employees to care for." As she finished her thought, she turned to him and placed her hand against the side of his face. "You are also a kind and unpretentious man; you seem to move through this world with a certain inner strength that most could only hope to have. All of that is on the inside of you—the person you are—but don't think for a moment I don't notice how handsome you are too!"

JD turned his face to kiss her hand but didn't stop there as he kissed her wrist, then her arm, and then her neck. Before kissing her on the lips, he smiled slyly and asked if she felt a shiver coming on. Kat didn't answer but instead beat him to the kiss. This time he put one hand on her lower back and pulled her toward his own body. And in doing so, he felt her quake.

CHAPTER 29

The last day of their adventure had arrived. They'd need to depart for the airport around siesta time, but on that Sunday morning, JD had arranged to take them to the outskirts of town where the small Baptist congregation gathered each Sunday under tents. Due to cooler morning temperatures, the service started around 8:00 a.m. and lasted two hours—something Kat was not used to, though she enjoyed what she could understand of the service. Besides, it gave her an opportunity to see JD worshipping God and being unashamed in the process. Being a Catholic, Barb had a very different experience in the service and replayed many of her observations in the truck as they drove back to the ranch to pack up and have an early lunch. One of the things Kat adored about her extroverted best friend was how unabashedly Barb shared her inner thoughts. It was as though Barb had no filter, but also no malice.

After a light lunch and goodbyes to both Carmen and Bernardo, the truck was packed up, and the ladies were headed back to the airport with JD. This time Kat came right out and asked JD about the gun she knew he was carrying, "Are you in danger, JD?"

Without hesitation, he assured her that he did not carry the gun because he felt he was in imminent danger, explaining, "Kat, this isn't Carmel. Mexico and Baja have their own unique set of issues. You need to know that in many ways, it's still like the Old West of America down here. I am not armed because I'm paranoid. I prefer to think of it as being prepared to defend myself, my property, and those I care about." Kat nodded in understanding as they turned onto the main highway.

The closer they got to the airport, the more talkative Barb became, while Kat became quieter as she contemplated having to say goodbye to JD. Before this trip, she'd thought of him as accessible, and the distance didn't seem insurmountable. Now, for some reason, she was beginning to sense that this parting would be a bit more wrenching. After all, they'd shared more of their hearts and lives with each other, and she didn't know when she'd see him again.

The goodbyes at the airport seemed to go as quickly as their few days in Sur Baja. Before she knew it, Kat was back in Pasadena thanking Barb for joining her on the trip and getting ready to make the drive home again. She and Barb had stayed up late the night before, and Kat confided in her friend that JD had expressed his feelings of love but that she'd not been able to respond to his question. Before Kat left to get in her car to depart that morning, Barb pulled Kat over to the mirror in the hall tree near the front door of the Beasley home. Barb had Kat stand in front of the mirror for a few seconds before saying, "Kat Steiner, look at that woman in the mirror. I'm telling you that is the look of a woman in love. I know you, Kat, and I've never seen you like this before, not even with Jason. In fact, I predict that the longer you are apart from JD, the more your heart will convince you of that love. Trust me."

Kat did look in the mirror, heaved a big sigh, and turned to Barb saying, "We shall see if you're right, Barb. I think I need to see Jason again to figure all this out. I'll keep you posted."

Kat drove home to Carmel on Labor Day, never stopping on the long drive. It was unusual for her not to get out at least once to stretch her legs, but Kat was deep in thought the entire trip. As she drove into her garage and headed into the empty house with her luggage, she felt a mixture of sadness and loneliness. There was no doubt that she missed JD, and even felt a twinge of guilt for being silent as he exposed his feelings for her. But she quickly corrected herself knowing that guilt should not be a factor in knowing her true feelings. She was determined to sort it out in her own mind...and soon.

Putting her things away, she began picking through the items in the fridge and cupboards to come up with something to eat. Though it hadn't rained, the day was overcast, and it seemed to reflect how she felt. As she ate her meal, she pulled out a pen and some paper from her junk drawer to make a list for the week ahead. She needed to do laundry, get groceries, get her business plans in order, send JD a thank you note, and pick up additional items she'd need to create that art piece for his place. But more importantly, she knew she must call Jason and tell him about JD.

CHAPTER 30

Though JD had been on vacation for the last several days, he was feeling like he'd made good progress in checking things off his list this first day back in the office. He was eternally grateful for Maria, his diligent assistant, who had everything in order for him upon return. Still, it was difficult to concentrate as his thoughts continually turned back to Kat as he replayed every moment he'd had with her over the previous days.

Maria had long since left for the day when JD was still in his office. Staring at the phone on his desk, he finally picked it up and dialed Kat's number. "Good evening, beautiful. How was your trip home?" he asked.

"Oh, JD, it's great to hear your voice. It all went smoothly, and I am just missing. . . I mean, finishing up some chores around the house," she responded.

JD went on to tell her, "That's funny; I was just finishing up some chores around the office, and I miss you too."

After the two spent a few minutes reminiscing about their time together, Kat thought she'd open up the subject of their relationship. This wasn't going to be easy for an introvert who, despite being an artist, was still a bit of a rational thinker. She thought she'd start by asking JD how he could be so sure that he loved her, because she wondered if perhaps she was overthinking an emotion that could not be explained rationally.

Kat could hear JD take a deep breath as he began to respond to her very big question. "Let me be clear that I've met numerous women over the years who were attractive or pleasant, or both, but none have caused me to go beyond myself. I'm not sure if that makes sense, but you have brought out something in me that I've never felt before, a feeling of not being complete when we are apart. I've just never known a woman who added to my life in such a way that I realized I was missing something. Or perhaps it is simply that God has opened my eyes to what I was missing when He brought you into my life."

Kat was fascinated by JD's explanation and piped in with her question, "So you felt something had changed, and that's how you knew?" When JD answered affirmatively, something resonated in Kat. Additionally, the fact that JD suggested divine leading reminded her that the Lord doesn't just lead one person in a relationship while keeping the other party in the dark about His will. She thanked JD for his thoughts, while in her heart she committed to being more sensitive to the Lord's leading in the matter. It was as though JD could see into her heart as he signed off with, "Believe me, Kat, I am praying for wisdom and discernment."

The next day Kat did send that thank you note to JD, made by hand, of course. She also spent the next several days at the shop getting things ready for opening. However, in the evenings, she'd work diligently in the back of the shop to create something for JD's home. It was on one of these days that she decided to call Jason.

"Kat, wow, you aren't usually the one to initiate a phone call. I was planning on calling you tonight anyway. So how did the Mexico trip go for you and Barb?" inquired Jason. Kat drew in a breath and began to explain the long story to Jason. She told him that the trip arose from an invitation from a gentleman she'd met on her trip to Europe. There was silence on the other end of the phone when she finished her last sentence. "Jason?" she finally voiced after several seconds past.

"I'm sorry, Kat, it's just that I didn't realize I had competition. Having said that, I know now that I'll just have to rise to the challenge so you don't get away!" said Jason. He went on to tell Kat that he was moving out of his parents' home and into his own apartment this weekend and wondered if she'd be willing to drive up to meet his parents and give him some decorating advice for the place. All Kat could feel was resistance: her own to the whole idea of the visit and Jason's to the notion that there could be some other man in Kat's life. She declined the offer, indicating she had too much work to do at the shop. With that, Jason gave her his new phone number but insisted that he'd call her again over the weekend.

She stayed busy all week and especially on Saturday. In part, she wanted to continue her work on JD's sculpture at the studio but also because she was avoiding taking Jason's call. As she spent the hours on the sculpture for JD, Kat just kept wondering if Jason really was concerned about having "competition" and even what his feelings for her really amounted to. He seemed sincere and even sincerely interested in pursuing her, but what exactly were his intentions? The more she labored over the artwork for JD, the more she realized that JD had been very clear about his feelings. At one point, she sat down to pray for clarity about her own feelings and those of these two suitors: one whom she felt she knew well from their history together and one whom she wanted to know more because of their recent history.

Arriving home later that evening, she made the decision not to wait for Jason to call her. Picking up the phone, she dialed his new number, which she had written on the notepad on the kitchen counter. When a female voice answered the phone, Kat was certain she must have written the number down incorrectly. She hesitatingly inquired, "Do I have the correct number for Jason Gabriel?" The voice on the other end didn't even respond. Instead, Kat could hear music in the background as the woman called for Jason to come to the phone. Kat strained to listen to what sounded like a party atmosphere. She still wasn't sure if she had the right number until she could faintly hear Jason's voice in the distance.

"So I've been seeing my old college flame off and on these days. She's a knockout, but even better, she's a trust fund baby." The comment was followed by a different male voice: "You're ridin' the gravy train then?" Muffled laughter followed as she could hear the phone scrape across what sounded like a countertop before Jason's voice came across with a simple, "Hello?"

"Hi, Jason, it's Kat. It sounds like I may have caught you at a bad time. We can talk another time."

"Oh, Kat, no, I was just…uh…just talking about you with some friends of mine who are over to check out the new place. Glad you called. What's up?"

"Oh, nothing really. Well, actually, I thought we might have a serious discussion about where things stood between you and me, but I think I already have my answer," Kat stated in a very matter-of-fact voice.

"Uh, you know, I'd like to have that conversation, Kat," Jason continued in a quieter voice. "Hey, tomorrow is Sunday, and I could drive down to meet you at church again. We'll talk. What do you say?"

Kat responded, "I say no, Jason. I wish you the best in your new place. Goodnight."

Hanging up the phone gently, Kat stood leaning over the kitchen counter for several minutes. She could feel the sting of tears starting to come on but fought them with all her might. Her mind raced to catch up with her emotions when she finally realized it wasn't sadness she felt; it was the pain of betrayal. While she thought Jason was someone who would always be authentic with her, she realized now that she was not much more than a meal ticket to him. That hurt.

Looking at the clock and seeing it was almost 9:00 p.m., Kat decided to take a long shower and then go to bed early. As she entered her bedroom, she sat down on the edge of her unmade bed, debating whether or not she'd shower or just crawl under the covers instead. In a flash of recollection, she remembered that she'd prayed just a few hours earlier for an answer to the questions she had about these two men. Though it had been a painful realization, she hung her head and whispered an audible, "Thank you, Lord, for answers. . .even the hard ones."

Just as she lifted her head, the phone on the nightstand rang out. Thinking it might be Jason, she hesitated as the phone rang a second and third time before she picked it up. Instead, it was JD who started out with "Katarina, I was a bit concerned that I might not catch you at home on a Saturday night."

Kat could tell that JD was fishing, so she was quick to respond. "I might not have been had I taken Jason up on his offer to meet his parents and help him move this weekend."

JD hesitatingly inquired, "Why didn't you go?"

Kat began to explain, "JD, do you recall that I told you I've never been in love before?"

"I certainly do remember that," responded JD.

She went on, "Yet when you asked me if I loved you, it dawned on me that perhaps I'd never wanted to be in love before. But therein is the difference in your case, JD. What's different is that everything in me wants to be in love with you. So, you see, something has changed for me too, and now I have that answer to your question. I do love you, Juan Diego Alvarez."

Kat could hear a sigh of relief on the other end of the phone, almost as if he'd held his breath through her entire declaration. Apparently wanting to confirm what he just heard, JD asked haltingly, "No more Jason then?"

Kat wanted to laugh at the question, but she sensed how serious JD was being in that moment, so she reported back, "No more Jason. I just want to see you again...and again." JD proceeded to tell her she'd have that "again" because he would be back in California later in the week and was hoping he could take her to dinner.

CHAPTER 31

The mid-September day had finally arrived, and Kat was looking forward to her dinner with JD. He would be flying from Los Angeles into Monterey, where she would pick him up at the small airport. She had made a reservation for them at a resort restaurant on the 17-Mile Drive. The place had great views of the golf course as well as the ocean. Kat had decided to dress up for this occasion, something she didn't often do. She even put in extra time to apply a bit of makeup and put her hair up, securing it with a sequined black clasp.

Having made it to the airport within minutes of JD's arrival time, she was definitely getting her exercise as she hurried to make it to his gate on time. As she made her way there, she could see the first passengers coming through the door. Relieved she hadn't missed anything, Kat stood patiently, though her heart was pounding in her chest. Somehow this visit felt different, because now she would be reunited with the man she knew she loved.

Finally, JD came through the door wearing a dashing European-cut dark suit and carrying a briefcase. His face lit up as he caught the sight of his gorgeous lady wearing high heels and the sexy dress he had encouraged her to buy in Paris. It didn't seem to matter to him that others were watching when he put his arm around her waist and planted a big kiss on her waiting lips. As he released her, he chimed in with, "It looks like a beautiful high-fashioned model has been sent to meet me at the airport. I do hope she'll allow me to escort her to dinner tonight."

Kat was still recovering from the kiss but responded, "It looks like a handsome businessman has stepped off an airplane to escort me to dinner tonight, and I can hardly wait!" With that, they made their way out of the airport and to her car.

The drive to the resort was beautiful, and the weather was acting more like summer than the nearing fall. With Kat in the driver's seat, she had a captive audience as she drove along the 17-Mile Drive showing JD all the lovely homes and views. When finally they arrived at the resort, JD hurried out of the car to open her car door for her and then placed her arm on his to walk her inside. "I want everyone to know you are with me," he said as he patted her hand now resting on his arm.

As the dinner courses were served, Kat and JD were talking business, family, horses, art, and more. At one point, Kat took a few minutes to tell JD that her last call with Jason had been last Sunday when he called her back. Though she didn't go into detail, she did say that she knew it wasn't the relationship for her—and she'd informed Jason that for the first time in her life she could truly say that she was in love. That seemed to bring the whole matter to a close for Jason, who went on to wish her the best in life.

JD put his utensils down and folded his arms across his chest and smiled saying, "I win the prize. So tell me, was it my big house and my money that convinced you?" Kat found herself laughing like she hadn't in over a year. JD had won her heart, and it had everything to do with who he was at the core of his being. He was loving, self-assured, patient, kind, and, as Barb would say, drop-dead gorgeous!

As they were finishing up the meal, JD excused himself from the table to make a brief phone call in the lobby but quickly returned. By the time he did, the waiter was arriving with a dessert for the two to share. Kat was surprised as the two hadn't placed an order for dessert. She gently inquired as to whether the waiter might be serving the wrong table. JD promptly noted that he had ordered it on his way back from the lobby, thinking it might be something she'd like.

The moment the waiter put the fluffy, white dessert in the center of the table, she knew immediately that it was something she'd like. For there on the top of the dessert was a beautiful three-stone diamond ring staring back at her. Kat could feel tears of joy coming to her eyes as she looked up at JD who was looking at her with his deep brown eyes. "I love you, and I will always want you in my life. Will you marry me, Katarina Steiner?" he asked.

Without hesitation, Kat answered, "Yes, JD, a thousand times, yes."

Chapter 32

JD had opted to stay at a hotel as close to Kat's home as he could get and didn't plan to return home until Sunday afternoon. That gave the newly engaged couple plenty of time to talk about the wedding plans. And there was so much to discuss that Kat was up early Saturday morning to collect JD at his hotel so they could start their day at a coffee shop in Carmel.

Over several cups of strong coffee and breakfast, the two were in their own world. Staring at each other and thrilled by the prospect of spending a lifetime together, it was now just a matter of how to make that official. JD opened the conversation with an offer to have the wedding at the ranch, though he knew that Kat had a church home in Carmel. Would she want a church wedding, or was she willing to have the ceremony outdoors? He was surprised that she immediately took him up on returning to the ranch for the wedding, largely because she knew the weather in Carmel to be so unpredictable in the fall.

"So you want to get married in the fall? And if so, do you mean this fall?" asked JD. Kat asked him if she might appear too eager if she told him she'd like to be his wife within weeks, not a year. "Wow, I like the sound of that!" he exclaimed. As they got deeper into the details, they realized the work that would go into pulling off a wedding in such short order. However, they concluded it could be done and set a date of November 15, just two months away.

After more conversation about the wedding itself, the discussion turned to where they would make their home. It was then that Kat learned that JD had dual citizenship and that their marriage in Sur Baja would be recognized in both countries. This conversation led to broader discussions of their various property holdings and investments. Though Kat was interested in living with JD in Todos Santos, JD wanted them to retain her Carmel property. The two talked about the potential to live anywhere in the world, given their global perspectives. However, they'd marry and live in Baja in the short-term while they considered their future endeavors.

Leaving the restaurant, they headed back to Kat's place to continue their planning. Arriving at home, Kat placed a call to Larry Barnes to see if he might be available to meet the two for lunch after church the next day before she had to take JD back to the airport. Larry picked up the phone after just one ring, and it startled Kat, but not enough to keep her from blurting out the news. "Larry, Kat Steiner here. And I've gotten engaged to be married!" said Kat. Larry was more responsive than she'd ever heard him before—excited, concerned, and just wanting to meet her intended. They established a time to rendezvous at the Old Fisherman's Grotto the next day at noon.

As Kat hung up the phone in the kitchen, JD pulled her to himself saying, "You know that I can still close my eyes and imagine you in your swimsuit, don't you?" Kat blushed and reminded him that she would never forget being held in his arms that day and seeing him bare-chested. Such talk soon led to intense kisses until JD stopped to suggest they'd better go walk on the beach to cool off.

Walking hand in hand, the two continued to make plans and talk about their "merger" of sorts, given all the financial matters that would need to be tended to by their respective advisors. In the middle of the conversation, Kat remembered that she had signed a one-year lease on a shop that she'd not be able to tend. JD injected, "Nothing to worry about. I have been meaning to add to my sales force, starting with a couple of salespeople in California who can work the American market. That will mean less travel for me. We'll convert it to workspace for those agents. Meanwhile, we need to figure out how to create space at the ranch for you to continue your artistic endeavors. Hey, perhaps I'll get to design and build a workshop just for you!"

With that, Kat turned to hug JD's neck as she whispered in his ear, "Thank you for thinking of me."

JD held her and tenderly stroked her long hair as he responded with, "Querida mia, besides wanting you to be my wife, I want you to be what God has gifted you to be, always."

As they turned to head back to her cottage, Kat asked JD if anyone back in Todos Santos knew what he was up to this weekend. JD let her know that Maria had booked his travel knowing it was his second trip to the area where Kat lived. "She has put it together," he said. "And I suspect she knows things are getting serious. Beyond that, there is no end to the not-so-subtle hints from Carmen and Bernardo. They don't know that I traveled here with your ring, but they recognize a man who is in love."

His comment reminded Kat of Barb's statements while she had Kat stand in front of that mirror. "Oh, JD, my best friend was right! Barb seemed to know I was in love with you even before I did. Now I can't wait to ask her to be my maid of honor at the wedding!" exclaimed Kat.

JD smiled and said, "Sounds like she and Antonio will be spending more time together because I'll be asking him to be my best man!"

CHAPTER 33

Sunday morning had Kat picking up JD at his hotel and heading to her church. The two had a great time worshipping together, and they even spent 30 minutes with the pastor in his study after the service. It was something he insisted upon when Kat introduced JD as her fiancé. Apparently, the pastor was feeling a bit paternalistic toward Kat, knowing her parents, who had been so instrumental in the life of the church, were gone. Pastor Summers spent a little time getting to know the two better, learned about their plans, and then prayed for their future together as man and wife.

As they drove toward Monterey to meet Larry for lunch, JD asked Kat how she felt about having his pastor officiate at their wedding. Kat had met Pastor Sanchez and was impressed with his kindness, though his English was limited. However, Kat knew that if they were to be wed in Todos Santos, she would have to turn many of those kinds of details over to JD to decide. She told him that they would have to stay in close communication over the next eight weeks to pull this off and that she would rely on him to make many of the arrangements. At best, she would be able to get a few friends there, but she acknowledged that most of the attendees would be people he knew. Therefore, Pastor Sanchez was the best choice.

Pulling into the parking space to head into the Old Fisherman's Grotto, JD seemed a bit nervous about this meeting. Kat asked him if he was okay, and JD remarked "Sure, it's just that meeting Larry, as you've described him, feels a bit like meeting your father. I have no one to ask for your hand in marriage, so I guess I feel like it's important that Larry approves."

Kat leaned over the center console in the car and kissed JD on the cheek saying, "Larry is a good judge of character, and you are of good character. If you weren't, I wouldn't have agreed to marry you!"

The lunch with Larry went well, and the three had great conversation about JD's history, family, home, and interests. Additionally, Larry was able to tell JD about Kat as a young girl growing up as the apple of her parents' eyes. There was some brief discussion about their business affairs, but Larry insisted that this was not the time for such things; he wanted to celebrate their love. However, he did take JD's business card and promised to make contact soon in order to get some sense of how the two wanted to proceed to combine their substantial financial holdings. He also offered to speak with JD's advisors as things moved along. But most importantly, Larry gave his blessing to the marriage, even praying for them before they parted ways.

With little time left to get JD to the airport, Kat had just one more thing to accomplish. She told JD that they needed to make a side trip to Seaside before he departed. He reminded her that she was in the driver's seat, so he was going wherever she wanted to take him. As they entered the town, she drove to the studio and parked directly in front of her shop. JD seemed puzzled but went along as Kat unlocked the front door and invited him in. Though the interior was still undergoing some finish carpentry work, Kat took JD's hand and led him to the studio in the back where he could barely see until she flipped on a single light that shone upon a workbench. There was but one solitary piece on the table, a breathtaking Spanish Mustang made of ceramic and artist resin. It stood about twenty inches high, and the details of the horse in a simple erect stance were stunning.

JD was momentarily speechless as he walked around the table to see the figure from every angle. Upon the horse was a cinnamon red bridle with matching Portuguese saddle. Mounted on a black matte base, it was an amazingly detailed piece of work that he could hardly take his eyes off of. When he was finally able to speak, Kat took over with, "He's yours, of course. I've been working on him most nights since I got back from Todos Santos. I hope you like it."

JD's voice cracked a bit as he returned to put his arms around her and held her tightly saying, "Kat, I more than like it; it's gorgeous. I will treasure it forever, though never more than I will treasure the artist."

With that he kissed her again and again on the lips, cheeks, and forehead. As she enjoyed his sweet caresses, they both seemed to forget about the sculpture as they continued to hold onto each other. As they kissed, Kat ran her hands up and down JD's strong arms. She secretly wondered what it might be like to be his sculptress. She concluded right then and there that she'd first need to memorize every part of him on their honeymoon.

As they made their way to the airport, Kat explained that she wasn't sure how to get the sculpture to the ranch, but she'd figure out a way, even if she had to carry it by hand on the plane. The two had accomplished much in the short time since JD had cleaned the dessert off the engagement ring and slipped it onto Kat's finger. Despite that, there was still so much to do and so many decisions to be made. They agreed to talk on the phone frequently to keep things moving toward their mid-November wedding date.

CHAPTER 34

Barb was screaming into the phone at Kat, "I told you so; I knew you were in love! Of course I'll stand with you at your wedding, Kat. That's what best friends are for! When is the date? How did Jason take the news?" Kat was barely able to get a word in edgewise for the din. However, when things settled down, Barb told Kat she'd have to ask her boss to find a substitute for the Friday before so she could fly down to be ready for the Saturday wedding. Kat made arrangements to see Barb the very next weekend so they could get caught up and go into Los Angeles to find dresses.

After hanging up the phone, Kat's mind came to a screeching halt. Not sure what to do to plan a wedding from this distance, she thought she'd better call a wedding planner to help her sort things out. Picking up the phone to contact someone out of the phone book, she recalled that Larry's eldest daughter was the wedding coordinator at his church. Digging around in her desk drawer, she found Olivia's card and dialed her number.

Olivia was thrilled to hear from Kat, and word had already traveled from her father about JD and the wedding, so it was just a matter of having lunch with Olivia the next day

147

in Monterey. While Kat knew she could tend to some of the details, she'd have to rely heavily on JD since his home was the venue. However, she also knew how busy he was with his many ventures, so she called him later in the evening. While they talked about the potential to have Olivia work with someone there, or even fly down to make arrangements, they spent more time talking about how much they missed and loved each other.

Meeting Olivia for lunch was something Kat was looking forward to. Olivia was about 10 years older than Kat. Growing up, Kat remembered how much she looked up to Olivia and thought she was so sophisticated. Olivia had now been married about eight years and had two young daughters. It had been quite a while since the two had spent any time together, so Kat was eager to catch up and to hear Olivia's wedding ideas.

When the two settled into their booth at the restaurant, Olivia had already heard from her babysitter about the six-year-old coming home early from school with a slight fever. Though a bit flustered from the news, Olivia was immediately focused on Kat and wanted to hear all about her intended. Kat told her how they met and about her trip to his home, and that they had just gotten engaged. Olivia was actually glad to hear that they had decided not to wait the nine to twelve months so many couples opted for just to plan a wedding. As she patted Kat's hand across the table, she reminded her that any wedding day will be memorable, but it's the lifetime they will build together that leaves its mark in this world.

Over their salads and iced tea, the two concluded that it would be important for Olivia to actually see the venue and to figure out what was locally available in the way of food, flowers, rental equipment, and entertainment. Kat wasn't sure how that would go over with Carmen, so she explained the situation and the fact that those who were caretakers spoke little or no English. Olivia laughed and said, "Katarina Steiner, you were such a little girl when I was your age, so you probably don't remember that I spent several summers on mission trips to Mexico and majored in Spanish in college!" Kat was embarrassed to admit that she didn't remember any of that about Olivia as most of her memories of Olivia started when she attended Olivia's wedding with her parents when Kat was only 12 years old.

Kat gave Olivia the address and phone number to reach JD and assured her that he could assist her with whatever she needed on that end. Olivia promised to call this week and figure out a time when she could get down to Sur Baja in the next seven to ten days or so. Thankfully, she had only one wedding at the church to deal with, and it was to be held in mid-October. As they finished up their time together, Olivia repeated back from her notes all the things Kat was hoping for in this wedding. As they parted, Olivia gave Kat a big hug and even called her "little sis."

CHAPTER 35

Among some of the decisions that Kat and JD made on the phone were about colors she had chosen, flowers, and the location for the ceremony. There was no doubt in Kat's mind that the large patio that faced the ocean would be the perfect place for this wedding. If it were cleared of everything, there would be enough space for many rows of chairs with an aisle down the center. And given the typical 75-85 degree weather in Todos Santos in November, they had an excellent chance of a perfect evening. They chose to hold the ceremony just after siesta time, 5:00 p.m., knowing that the sun would be setting over the ocean as the ceremony came to a close. That just left the details of feeding and entertaining the guests, which they'd leave to the wedding planner, who could consult with Carmen.

With all the details starting to feel a bit overwhelming, Kat decided that the way to keep calm and centered was to keep a diary of these days leading up to the wedding. On this day, she pulled out an old steno pad she found in the desk. She grabbed a pen and got comfortable on the living room sofa to start capturing her thoughts about the engagement and these first days. Opening the cardstock cover of the spiral notebook, her heart skipped a beat as she saw her mother's handwriting on the pages. Was this Liesl's diary that she had stumbled across? No, it appeared to be in list form, with space below each numbered item. Item number one was her father's name, followed by the words, "health, testimony, and wisdom." Item number two was her name, Katarina, followed by the words, "a gentle spirit, discernment, the man of God's choosing." As Kat read the words, the tears started to come on as she realized that she had found her mother's prayer list and that her mother had been praying for her future spouse even while Kat was still in college.

The words on the page were blurred from the tears in her eyes, so Kat closed the notebook and set it down on the coffee table. She knew her mother was a praying woman, but Kat was in awe of how strategic those prayers were. She sent up her own prayer that the Lord would tell her parents about the man of His own choosing and how happy she was that JD had chosen her. She knew that JD's parents had had a good marriage and that her own parents had been happily married for decades. As she continued her prayers, she sought the blessings of God by making her own strategic ask, "May our marriage also be a model to our children, should you grant us that gift. Amen."

CHAPTER 36

Kat drove to Pasadena on Friday afternoon so she could stay at Barb's house that night. They both wanted to get an early start on dress hunting in L.A. the next day. As the friends tried on dresses, conferred with each other, and talked about the wedding, they grew increasingly excited about Kat's big day.

Of course, a big part of the excitement was the hunt for the wedding dress. Kat knew she was looking for something with a Latin flair and pretty Spanish lace, and by the end of the day, she had found it. Barb had also found a very exciting dress that Kat thought might be perfect for the look she wanted to capture in this wedding.

As it turned out, the dresses they chose needed no alterations. However, Kat knew she was going to have to search a bit further for her veil and shoes. And of course, there was the matter of JD's wedding band. These things were items she'd check around for in both Santa Barbara on her route home and Monterey over the following week.

With Barb being her only attendant, Kat was wondering if she might have put JD in an awkward spot owing to the fact that he had three brothers. She figured she'd better check in with him on that when next they spoke by phone. In any case, she'd need to contact Olivia as well to let her know how things were coming together on her end.

Driving home via Santa Barbara, Kat stopped to check out a store she liked that carried shoes and accessories. Wandering around the store, the shop owner asked her if there was something in particular that she was hoping to find. Kat told her she hoped to find shoes to go with her wedding dress, and the owner excused herself to retrieve a pair from the back that Kat might consider. The shopkeeper returned with a lovely pair of white heels in Kat's size. As she tried them on and looked at them in the mirror, she concluded they would be perfect with the dress. Telling the woman that she'd take the shoes, as they made their way to the counter, Kat noticed a beautiful pair of white pearl drop earrings. As she picked them up, the owner told her they were authentic and therefore a bit pricey. Kat turned over the box they were sitting in and could see the price tag. She thought twice about buying them but concluded they were to be the only jewelry she'd wear on her wedding day, outside of her engagement ring and the wedding ring that JD would place on her finger. "I'll take them, along with the shoes, please," announced Kat.

Back in the car after making her purchases, Kat turned around to look again at her beautiful wedding dress lying across the small space in the back of the vehicle. She was having no regrets with the purchases she'd made thus far. Driving back onto the road homeward, Kat was starting to look beyond the wedding as she considered what life with JD in Todos Santos might be like. Would she like living there? Would they live there for the rest of their lives together or return to the United States at some point? So many questions, but the unknown future didn't seem to concern Kat at all, as long as she would spend that future with her beloved.

CHAPTER 37

As the weeks passed, the details of the wedding were coming together in Carmel and in Todos Santos. There was no doubt that Kat was getting things done, though the hardest part was putting a halt to the business plans with the shop. Since she had talked it through with JD, however, she was pleased to know that the place would come in handy. She sold the pottery wheels, but otherwise left things pretty much as they were. Hearing about Kat and JD's intent to repurpose the space for inside sales people, Jim Dixon also seemed fine with the plan, while wishing her and her fiancé all the best.

The wedding invitations were sent, with most of the attendees likely to be friends and family of JD. However, Kat had invited the Beasleys, the Barnes tribe, and several friends from college and her church. She felt a bit guilty mailing off invites to her relatives in Vienna, knowing they wouldn't be able to come. However, she had already sent a long letter to her grandparents to explain how happy she was and that she understood the distance and cost might make it difficult for them to attend. To Annika, she sent a photo of the sculpture she had made for JD, along with a letter that she'd hoped would cause her aunt to understand that she was marrying a man who had made it clear to her that she wasn't just the next thing, or even just another thing. Kat told Annika that she'd found someone for whom she was the one and only thing, just as he was to her.

JD and Kat had included in their invitations a specific request that attendees not bring or send wedding gifts. They had drafted a paragraph that was printed on the back of their invites that simply stated that the couple had no need of things, just the love of friends and family along with their promise to uphold the marriage in prayer. They did, however, include the address of a California-based organization that was heavily involved in international relief work, with a particular focus on children. There was a deep famine in Ethiopia, which was all over the news, so Kat and JD wanted to encourage people to give to that effort instead of them. Additionally, and privately, the couple had pooled their own resources to make a large donation.

With just four weeks until the Saturday evening wedding, Olivia and Kat had made some final decisions before Olivia traveled to the ranch and met JD, Carmen, and Bernardo. Apparently, she had been quite a hit since she was fluent in their language and that made the planning go very smoothly. One of the bits of news Olivia brought back to Kat was that JD had officially asked Antonio to be his best man and his brother had agreed. JD's older brothers would then be free to be with their wives and children during the wedding. Kat was feeling a bit of relief over this decision, particularly in light of the fact that Barb and Antonio already knew each other.

As it turned out, Olivia learned that Carmen was very interested in preparing much of the food. Kat was surprised because she had thought Carmen might like to have a break from working in the kitchen to just enjoy the wedding. However, Olivia told Kat that Carmen was definitely the mothering type who wouldn't be able to enjoy the wedding without feeling she'd made a contribution. Given that, Olivia had asked Carmen to make the wedding cake, Mexican wedding cookies, and even a homemade piñata for the children who would be in attendance. Carmen had agreed and characterized all of it as her wedding gifts to Katarina and JD.

Beyond the wedding to be held on the large patio, Olivia had indicated that there would need to be a bit of an intermission period after the ceremony when the chairs could be placed around long tables that would be brought in for the reception in the same location. Kat and Olivia concluded that with approximately 100 people in attendance, they would encourage guests to depart the patio by initially putting the musicians at the front of the estate where there would be small round tables, chairs, and lantern lights strung overhead. The hors d'oeuvres and drinks would be served there while the patio was being transformed for dinner and dancing. These were all details that Olivia would have to arrange through Carmen, JD, and, to a certain extent, his assistant, Maria.

After a particularly busy day of planning, it was now late evening on a night when JD had agreed to call Kat to make some other last minute decisions. When the phone rang, as usual Kat's heart raced as she reached for the phone next to her bed. With her head on her pillow and the handset to her ear, she told JD about her day. He reciprocated and updated her on the plans being handled there. It seemed the thing on JD's mind this week had been getting some landscape workers out to the ranch to spruce up the place. He also wanted to assure Kat that Maria had taken on the task of ordering the flowers and making sure they were delivered as Olivia had specified.

But once the business of the day was discussed, they could escape into each other again. They both had dreams and hopes for their future together. They also had so much more to learn about each other. Then, before saying their goodbyes on these frequent calls, JD would often ask again, "Kat, do you love me?" This night she told him that she'd never stop loving him.

CHAPTER 38

The week of her wedding had arrived, and Kat was trying to figure out what to have shipped to the ranch versus what she should take in her luggage. Her dress and other items for the wedding day were things that Olivia planned to take with her as she'd be arriving a few days before the wedding. The real question for Kat was what she should take with her in light of the fact that she'd now be making her home in Todos Santos. She was once again preparing to shut down the home in Carmel for a season, even though she and JD were still thinking of it as a vacation home. She knew she'd be returning at some point but trying to decide what she wanted to take to her new primary residence was tricky.

Though many of the friends of the bride would be arriving the day of the wedding and staying overnight in La Paz, some of JD's family would be staying at the ranch. JD's oldest brothers, César and Pablo, would be with their wives and children, so the household would be buzzing. The more difficult part would be to keep the bride and groom apart on the wedding day, as Kat would be flying in the day before the wedding. However, JD had assured her that he'd honor that tradition by sequestering himself until the evening ceremony.

161

In the days leading up to her flight to La Paz, Kat thought about how much of the wedding felt like it was out of her control. She caught herself wondering how many surprises she'd encounter in her own wedding! It made her very grateful for the organizational skills and savvy of Olivia, who had made this process so easy for Kat. She couldn't imagine what it might take to coordinate a wedding held in another country. On the other hand, she thought, how easy the details of the honeymoon would be given that JD's villa was like a resort that they wouldn't want to leave. And the thoughts of a honeymoon with JD just made it all the more difficult to stay focused on her final tasks in Carmel.

CHAPTER 39

For once Kat had chosen a window seat on the airplane. She wanted to be able to see La Paz coming into view as she touched down on this Friday before her wedding day. Once again, JD would be there to greet her, but this time it would be just the two of them. He promised to take her to lunch in town and then whisk her away to her new home. He wanted to give Kat an opportunity to meet his brothers and their families, who were already at the ranch. But he also wanted to see that she had time with Olivia and Carmen to discuss all the last minute details.

Kat was so excited about the wedding but desperate to see her fiancé. As she walked down the shiny metal staircase from the plane onto the hot tarmac, she could hardly wait to pass through the preliminaries to see JD on the other side of those doors. The processing seemed to take even longer this time, but she endured it all knowing it would not be much longer until she could rest in his arms.

As she walked through the doors being propped open by an airport worker, there waiting directly in front of her was her handsome, brown-eyed man. As she hurried over to his embrace, she realized that something was different about him. It wasn't something she could immediately discern, but the moment he kissed her she realized he had cut his long hair. As she met his kisses, her hand reached up to the back of his neck where she verified what she had seen with her eyes. As he released her, he asked, "Surprised?"

Still in his embrace, she leaned back, and he must have seen the approval in her eyes as she ran her fingers through his thick, brown hair. "A bit surprised, but I swear, it wouldn't matter what you did; you just get better looking every time I see you!" said Kat.

The two headed to pick up the bags and then to his Bronco. Once back in the vehicle, JD leaned over again to kiss Kat lightly. Staring at her for a moment, he finally spoke, as if to himself, saying, "Juan Diego, you are a blessed man to have such a stunning beauty return your love and say yes to your proposal of marriage."

Kat smiled and responded with her own self-talk, "And, Katarina Steiner, what did you ever do to deserve such a manly specimen who wants to marry you?" They laughed at themselves for the silliness of it all yet cherished the moment as a reminder of just how fitted for each other they were.

Lunch was filled with chatter about the wedding tomorrow, the family, the guest list, the food, the music, and more. As much as Kat was enjoying it all, she could not get past the intense physical attraction she felt for JD. He, too, must have been feeling it for he hardly ate much on his plate and even moved himself closer to her in the half-round booth where they had been seated. As they waited to pay the bill, he put one hand on her leg under the table. Kat could feel her temperature rising at his touch. In that moment, she wondered out loud if this was why the tradition of not seeing each other for 24 hours before the wedding was started.

JD laughed and then leaned over to whisper in her ear, "I feel like a kid on Christmas Eve who just wants to open his presents now."

CHAPTER 40

As Kat and JD pulled onto the property, they could see his niece and nephews kicking a ball around the circular driveway. As he parked, the three were converging on the truck to greet JD and meet his bride-to-be. As Kat got out of the vehicle, the children were lining up to see her. JD came around to introduce them all. Arturo and Anarosa were the children of César, and Gabino was Pablo's son. Kat asked each of them how old they were, and in order, they responded in Spanish, "Ocho, cinco, and cuatro." The children were precious and full of energy. Anarosa was hopping from one foot to another, eagerly asking JD why they couldn't have the wedding today. Kat understood her question but blushed at JD's answer when in Spanish he responded, "Why, I'd love to have it today—and start the honeymoon tonight!"

Then JD scooped up Gabino in his arms only to hear the little one ask in Spanish, "What's a honeymoon?"

Kat smiled at JD and said, "Go on, you got yourself into this one!"

Antonio was making his way to the car to help JD carry Kat's bags but not without stopping to give her a big hug. No sooner had he reached to pick up her suitcase than the rest of her new family members appeared in the driveway. Kat was introduced to Pablo and his wife, Norma. Then she met César and his wife, Amparo. They were all so welcoming, and the two women quickly latched onto Kat's arms to walk her into the house, while the men talked and stopped to kick the ball around with the children. By the time Kat made it into the house, she looked back to see JD coming through the small courtyard carrying Anarosa in one arm while juggling one of Kat's suitcases in the other. He seemed so comfortable around children, and they seemed to adore their uncle.

With all the chatter in the hallway, in Spanish no less, Kat wondered if she'd ever get to a point where she could sort it all out. Right now, it was a din that she could only make occasional sense of. It was a relief to see Olivia coming out of the kitchen area to greet her...and help translate! The first order of business was to get Kat settled in the same room she had occupied on her first visit, with Olivia in the adjoining bedroom. The theater room had been converted into sleeping quarters for Antonio and the two boys, while Anarosa would be with her parents in the master suite. Pablo, Norma, and Gabino were across the hallway from Olivia, while Carmen retained her own room rights. Amidst all the noise of children and chatter, Kat could see Antonio, Pablo, and César walking JD back outside. She momentarily panicked as she realized she might not see him again until the wedding, a fact that Olivia confirmed, informing Kat that he'd be relegated to the stable apartment with Bernardo for the next 24 hours.

CHAPTER 41

Dinner was light fare and held in the formal dining room, but it seemed so odd to Kat that JD wasn't present in his own home. Instead, Carmen had earlier sent the children down to the stable to deliver meals to JD and Bernardo. Olivia held court in the dining room as she was the one person who could translate for Kat and answer her many questions about tomorrow.

Kat learned that most people would arrive around 4:30 p.m., and the wedding would start promptly at 5:00 with opening music, a guitar instrumental piece that Antonio had written for the wedding. Kat was already thanking Antonio for the wedding gift of his music. Olivia also reminded the children around the table that they must get a good night's sleep and be on their best behavior for the wedding. Kat couldn't help but sense that the admonition was probably falling on deaf ears!

Insisting on helping Carmen clean up after dinner, Kat also helped her and Olivia set things out for breakfast in the morning. Olivia and Carmen also went into the details of the food that would be provided for the guests. Apparently, long tables would be set up end to end and covered with white linens. This was to promote family style eating and allow the hired event staff to serve food in large portions to be passed around by the guests.

Olivia also walked Kat out to the patio to see the rows of white chairs already set in place. With one chair missing from the inside of the front row, there was in its place a wheelchair. Olivia explained that it was the wheelchair JD's father occupied for the last several years of his life. JD had requested it be placed there to represent all four of their missing parents.

Along the center aisle she would walk was the rose-red on white satin runner. There was also a beautiful, black wrought iron archway structure at the end of the patio that would be wrapped in white fabric and red roses. This is where the ceremony would take place. As Kat looked at all the preparations, she turned to Olivia to tell her how happy she was with everything. With a combination of relief, fatigue, emotion, and nerves, Kat felt herself on the verge of tears. Olivia gave her a big hug and then turned Kat's attention to the darkened western horizon, and she promised her a beautiful sunset tomorrow evening, just as they were saying, "I do."

As the two ladies came back in the house through the kitchen, Kat caught some of the chatter that Carmen was directing at Olivia. They were talking about the cake, so Kat asked to see it. Olivia told Kat that Carmen would add the finishing touches tomorrow but didn't want Kat to see it until the reception. So now Kat understood what the word *sorpresa* meant; it was to be a surprise! Kat went over to Carmen and reached for her hand saying, "Muchas gracias, Carmen." Carmen waved her free hand before her eyes and then reached for the handkerchief she had in her pocket to wipe away the tears. It was a precious moment that cemented their relationship.

Kat could feel her exhaustion and said her goodnights to everyone. As she and Olivia headed off to their respective rooms, they discussed final plans for tomorrow. Before they made the turn down the hall of bedrooms, Kat could hear the short-step padding of little feet behind her. Turning around, they saw little four-year-old Gabino running after them. Looking up at Kat with his big brown eyes, Gabino began fishing something out of his pocket. Finally pulling out a crumpled piece of paper, he proudly announced that his uncle had given it to him when the children took some food down to the stable. He held out the note for Kat to take, which she did while kneeling down to Gabino's level. "Muchas gracias, Gabino," said Kat, which just caused the rather shy little one to turn and dash back down the hall.

As Kat's head hit the pillow on this night, she stared out the skylight above her head to see the bright stars against the inky sky. She could hardly believe it was now just hours before she'd be Mrs. Alvarez. Now alone, she carefully unfurled the handwritten note Gabino had remembered to deliver from JD. It read very simply:

> *Dear Katarina:*
>
> *My last night as a single man holds no sentimentality for me because I can't wait to build a life with you in marriage. The Cornerstone is set for us by God, and tomorrow we start building together. Kat, you know that my love for you came early in the relationship, but I want you to know that it will stay late—to the end of time, in fact. May you sleep well tonight knowing that there isn't anything you can do to make me love you more, and nothing you could do to cause me to love you less.*
>
> *JD*

CHAPTER 42

While it had been a bit difficult to fall asleep last night, Kat did get eight solid hours of sleep before her long eyelashes fluttered open to the excitement of her wedding day. It didn't take long to get out of bed to check the clock and make her way to the bathroom. Now 8:00 a.m., there was some evidence that Olivia had already been in the shower and out of the bathroom. Kat was feeling a bit guilty for having slept in. However, as she went back to her room, there was a knock on the door with Olivia's voice asking Kat if she could come in. "Please do," responded Kat.

Olivia entered the room to announce that she had Kat's dress and other items in her room and they needed to transfer them over to her bedroom through their adjoining bathroom. Kat followed Olivia over to her room, and hanging on the back of her door was Kat's wedding dress. She hadn't seen it in a while, and it took her breath away to see it now. She fell in love with it all over again as she admired the beautiful white gown with its puffed silk fabric at the shoulders, tapering off to laced long sleeves. And the train of the dress was long and rounded off with the lace pattern. Next to the dress, draped over a chair, was the beautiful gauzy veil with the same lace pattern around the edges that would frame her face. Yes, there was no doubt it was stately and classic, while still just low cut enough and almost off the shoulder enough to show off some of her best assets.

Kat was caught up in the moment, until she realized that she was still in her pajamas and looked like morning. Once she and Olivia made the transfer and went over the checklist to make sure Kat had everything in her room she'd need to get ready for the wedding, it was time for her to get cleaned up and have some breakfast. Olivia told her she'd meet her in the dining room for coffee in 30 minutes.

Kat made her way down to the dining room within the 30 minutes, wondering why the household seemed so quiet. When she arrived in the dining room, she could see there were already covered trays of Mexican wedding cookies lining the side tables.

She sat down next to Olivia, who was talking to Antonio. Kat couldn't make out exactly what they were saying but could tell it had something to do with the music for the wedding. While they finished their conversation, Kat poured herself some coffee and reached for one of the rolls and the bowl of jam. Saying a brief prayer over her food, she realized that she was very hungry. In his stilted English, Antonio asked Kat, "How do you feel today, Katarina?"

She smiled and attempted her answer in Spanish, "Nervioso, pero feliz."

Antonio laughed and said, "I, too, would be nervous and happy on my wedding day!"

As Kat was eating breakfast, she asked where everyone was this morning as she knew the household couldn't be this quiet with the children around. Olivia told her that she'd sent all the children with Pablo and Norma to Todos Santos to pick up some of the last minute items that were needed. According to Olivia, it was part of the plan to keep the children occupied today. However, she also wanted them rested a bit before getting them cleaned up and ready for the wedding at 5:00 p.m. She reminded Kat that the same went for her; she was to be occupied with helping Carmen and her this morning, then resting, and then spending the last few hours before the wedding getting ready. Her job was to look beautiful and be ready to walk down the aisle with Olivia's father, Larry Barnes, who would be arriving just one hour before the wedding.

CHAPTER 43

As Barb finished applying Kat's makeup, all that was left for Kat to do was slip into her wedding dress. Kat could hear the din of voices growing stronger outside her door as guests were arriving. "Oh, Barb, I always dreamed of my wedding day, and here we are!" said Kat as she positioned the neckline and sleeves of her dress.

Barb had a big grin on her face as she stepped back to look at Kat standing five foot eleven inches tall with her heels on. "You look gorgeous, Kat...like a Spanish queen! I can't wait to put that veil on for you, but first you need put the final touches on your hair and makeup," said Barb.

Barb was already dressed and ready to walk down the aisle with Antonio as soon as he finished playing the introductory song that he had written for this wedding. Barb told Kat that the band was in place just off to the left corner of the patio. She reminded Kat that she had JD's ring and even showed Kat that she was wearing it on her thumb and it would be hidden as she carried the white rose bouquet with that hand. It seemed everything was in place, though there were definitely some nerves as Kat jumped in with, "Wait, where are my flowers? What did we do with those?"

Barb just smiled and reassured her that they were on the dresser right where Olivia had placed them.

At 4:45 p.m., Barb placed the veil on Kat, who had to bend down a bit as her best friend was several inches shorter than her. Barb then corrected her earlier statement by saying, "Now you look like a Spanish queen who is going to mass!" Once all the adjusting was done, Kat took Barb's hand and squeezed it, but she couldn't get out a word for fear of crying. Barb just looked at Kat and said, "I know; best friends just know. Now, I'll see you out there. You're gonna blow them all away because this is one runway you were meant to walk!"

Out on the patio, the guests were arriving and being seated in the white chairs facing the wrought iron arch that now looked like a red and white rose trellis. Beyond that, the sun was hanging low over the Pacific Ocean. At exactly 5:00 p.m., Antonio took a seat with the band and began playing the bold but beautiful guitar music he had written.

As the audience hushed to listen to the music being played on the patio, JD was walking El Jefe out from the stable at the south side of the ranch. The black horse's mane was braided with red ribbons, and he was perfectly groomed. JD mounted his horse and followed the trail to the beach, an exercise that calmed his nerves on this evening as he made his way alone to his wedding. Once he made his way to the beach, he could see the people seated on the patio in the distance.

Turning to the right and moving El Jefe at a faster pace, JD headed toward the patio. As he drew closer to the patio, he could hear the faint music growing louder. JD could see Bernardo waiting off to the side of the villa, prepared to take El Jefe and tie him up on the other side of the house. Bernardo was dressed in traditional black drawstring pants, white shirt, black jacket, and red string tie. Riding up to the patio, JD stopped El Jefe and had the large horse rear up once before settling down again. The crowd clapped at the flashy entrance then watched JD dismount and hand the reins to Bernardo.

As JD stepped onto the patio, he made his way over to Pastor Sanchez, who was standing under the archway. The two men shook hands as Antonio and the band concluded the introductory song. The band then began another beautiful instrumental song as Antonio made his way into the house to collect Barb so they could walk down the aisle first.

Within minutes, Barb emerged in her short, rose-red dress that was slightly off her shoulders, which were covered with a matching fringed-lined shawl. She was carrying her baby red and white roses in one hand and had her arm wrapped around Antonio's arm as they slow-walked the aisle. As the two approached the front, they peeled off to stand on their respective marks. JD shook Antonio's hand, but his eyes were fixed on the doors to the patio where he knew his bride would soon appear.

As Kat appeared in the doorway with Larry as her escort, JD never took his eyes off of her. The music became even more dramatic for her entry, and she took a deep breath as Larry patted her hand that rested on his arm. Everyone was now standing, and she was starting to feel like the Spanish queen that Barb had mentioned. She could see Anarosa in her pretty pink dress standing next to her older brother. She couldn't help but notice little Gabino in a precious white three-piece suit with red tie and cummerbund, and she also couldn't help but wink at him.

As she and Larry drew closer to the front, Kat stopped at the wheelchair and bent down slightly to place her bouquet of deep red baby roses on the chair. As she did, her eyes caught a glimpse of Carmen, who was already wiping away a tear from her eye. Kat had to look away so she didn't start tearing up herself.

With just a few more steps, Larry placed her hand on JD's arm, and he led his beautiful bride to stand before the minister. Kat could see the photographer snapping pictures of her as she came down the aisle, but she was hoping he got plenty of photos of her handsome groom. JD was wearing a black suit, white shirt, and rose-red vest with matching tie. She momentarily glanced downward to see he was also wearing highly polished black cowboy boots, and that made her smile inside and out.

The ceremony began and ended with prayer, just as the two had requested. They also took their first communion together, and Pastor Sanchez even asked the audience to publicly commit to supporting the couple in their married life together by answering, "We will." When finally the moment came to exchange rings, Kat was shaking as she and JD each said "I do"–first in English, then in Spanish. And as the sun was dipping below the vast blue ocean in the distance, the pastor pronounced them man and wife, "Señor y la Señora Alvarez!" As he did, JD reached over to take Kat in his arms and dip her across his body in dramatic fashion as he kissed her. As she came up from the dip, the crowd erupted in clapping and cheers! Once again, while Kat felt she'd been a bundle of nerves, JD seemed so relaxed.

As if that kiss weren't enough drama, Kat noticed that Bernardo was standing just off the patio holding the reins of El Jefe. JD pointed toward the horse, knowing Kat was unsure of what he was planning. Bernardo assisted JD as he got on the horse, and then both Bernardo and JD lifted Kat to sit in front to ride sidesaddle. With his muscular arms squeezing her to hold her in place, he assured her that she was safe and then he waved to the crowd. Turning the horse toward the water, they quite literally rode off into the sunset.

Getting over her initial fears of riding bareback on El Jefe, she let herself relax, and JD could feel her relying on his arms and leaning into him. "Mrs. Alvarez, you are the most beautiful bride the world has ever seen. And I am the most blessed man in the world to call you mine," JD whispered in her ear as they watched the sun slip below the horizon. Kat turned to kiss JD, and she could feel the horse slowing down a bit without JD's full attention.

As the newlyweds reached the water's edge, JD turned El Jefe northward, which prompted Kat to ask where he was taking her. "In the weeks leading up to the wedding, I put my mind to that little cabin up the beach. Barb was right; it needed a bathroom, so I extended the roofline and added one. That, my dear Kat, will be our honeymoon suite," announced JD. He went on to say, "Beyond your wedding ring, a cabin addition may not be much of a gift, but we can return to it anytime you like." Kat's heart was pounding as she kissed JD again and again, stopping only to tell him how happy she was. Again El Jefe was walking very slowly due to neglect, but once the kisses ended, JD put pressure on the horse to move more quickly toward the cabin.

Upon arrival, JD slipped off the horse and reached up to grab Kat by the waist to help her down. He tied up the horse by the side of the cabin and returned to open the door for Kat. Once inside, Kat noticed that the place had been fixed up, dressed with a vase of fresh flowers, a single lit lantern on the dresser, and even their clothing for the reception was hanging on the front of the new bathroom door.

As she was looking around the cabin, JD took off his jacket and vest and then proceeded to loosen his tie. He then asked her if he could help her out of her wedding dress. Feeling her cheeks flushing red, she removed her veil and draped it over the only chair in the room. She then turned her back on JD to explain how to remove the train—something he was eager to do. Once that was off, he began to unzip the dress as Kat slipped off her heels. As JD helped her remove the dress, his eyes beheld her standing there in her sexy white bra and panties. After a few seconds of silence, he lowered his voice to whisper to her that they might be late to the reception. Kat just nodded and began unbuttoning his shirt to reveal that bare chest she couldn't wait to touch again.

JD began kissing Kat deeply and nonstop, as she continued to urgently undress him. As JD moved her toward the canopy bed, the two were fueled by passion and love for one another, and it didn't take long for them to consummate the marriage. As the contented couple then lingered in each other's arms, Kat told JD she didn't know if she wanted to leave the cabin to go to the reception. "I want more of you, Kat... and agree that this release of tension will only be temporary," JD responded. "However, we need to remember that we have a lifetime together, so thanking our guests and having a meal with them is what we must do now," he continued.

Kat agreed but followed up with a sigh saying, "You're right. But let's come back to the cabin as soon as possible!"

With a gleam in his brown eyes, JD just said, "That sounds like a plan, pretty lady."

CHAPTER 44

Kat and JD changed into less formal clothing for the reception and returned to the house the same way they departed. Along the way, Kat was able to thank JD for the note that contained such a beautiful expression of unconditional love. By the time they arrived, they could see that the patio had been transformed for dinner. The tables lined the squared off U-shape of the patio, leaving a dancing space in the center. After JD tied up El Jefe, the couple walked through the house to the small patio in the front of the villa. There were small lanterns strung overhead as they passed through their friends and family, who were shaking JD's hand and hugging Kat in congratulations. The children of friends and family were already out front taking turns swinging away at the piñata that Carmen had made for them.

As the two made their way through the crowd, Kat's eyes searched for Barb. Finally spotting her by searching for the darling red dress she wore for the wedding, Kat noticed that Antonio had her all to himself in the far corner of the driveway. Kat tugged on JD's sleeve to get his attention and pointed in the direction of Barb and Antonio. He looked over and laughed out loud, saying that he'd never really thought of his brother as a "ladies man," but perhaps there was hope for him after all!

Within 30 minutes of their arrival, Bernardo was ringing a bell that hung on a side wall of the small patio. That was the signal for everyone to head back to the large patio for dinner. This time Kat and JD walked around the villa instead of cutting through the house, and most followed their lead. The children, however, were still attempting to break open the piñata, and their mothers had to round them up.

As everyone arrived to sit at the tables, the servers were already placing beautiful platters on the tables. They were filled with bowls of lobster bites, cooked spicy shrimp, rice, and beans. There were also plates of perfectly prepared pacific snapper and shark steaks. To drink were bottles of both rosa and blanco "Spanish champagne" known as cava. And, of course, with all of this came the endless tortillas, shredded pork, and fresh salsa. As the guests arrived, Pastor Sanchez asked everyone to quiet down so he could pray over the meal, and as soon as the "amen" was said, the chatter erupted again.

Kat and JD sat at the head table with the rest of the wedding party. As they were digging in, JD elbowed Kat and nodded down the table toward Barb to see Antonio talking to her. Just before taking his first bite, he chuckled and asked Kat if Barb was learning Spanish or just staring at Antonio as his lips flapped! Kat nudged him back and came back with, "Well, you realize it wouldn't have mattered to me what you said in the Louvre that day, I would have followed you anywhere."

As he leaned back in his chair and put his arm around her, JD responded, "That was just the risk I had to take. And look how it paid off!"

As the noise levels grew and the food started to disappear, the band returned to their corner to start playing again. Their first number was clearly designed to get people on the dance floor—a rousing version of El Jarabe Tapatìo, the Mexican Hat Dance! Kat looked over to see Carmen leaning up against the wall, but she had lifted her long skirt a bit, and her feet were tapping already. The crowd seemed to be calling for something, and JD leaned over to tell her that they wanted the two of them to initiate the dance. Standing up, he took her by the hand and ushered Kat into the center of the patio. As he did, Kat noticed that the guests began gathering in a ring around them as JD put his hands behind his back and began slowly showing Kat the dance steps. She had to improvise as she didn't know anything about this dance, but the crowd clapped approvingly.

JD pointed out to her that it was a tradition in Mexico for the guests to form the shape of a heart as they encircle the couple. As she looked around, she could see that was the case, but then JD encouraged everyone to join in. It didn't take long for Carmen to start swaying around Bernardo who had his hands behind his back now too. Just as people were joining in the dance, eight-year-old Arturo ran through the middle of the crowd with the big, red, heart-shaped piñata that now had a gaping hole in the side. Anarosa, Gabino, and the other children were following him and picking up pieces of candy that were falling out. The entire sight made Kat laugh as she fell into JD's arms.

Well into the night the friends and family ate, drank, and watched JD and Kat cut the beautiful cake that Carmen had made. She was so proud of her multi-layered lemon cake frosted in white and covered with red roses of frosting. And it tasted as good as it looked. The mountains of Mexican wedding cookies were fabulous too. The whole party continued past midnight, but Kat and JD made their escape at about 11:00 p.m., just about the time some of the extended family were setting off fireworks down at the beach. Of course, the newlyweds hardly noticed any of that upon returning to the cabin for their own fireworks.

CHAPTER 45

The morning brought another beautiful day on the beach, with sunlight streaming through one of the small windows of the cabin. Kat woke before JD and snuggled up close to his chest. That caused him to moan while patting her on the top of the head. "Good morning, my sweet," he said. Kat started to move to get out of bed, but he grabbed her arm and asked her where she was going.

"To the new bathroom you built, of course! I thought I could at least brush my teeth and look a bit more presentable for you this morning," she responded. JD loosened his grip and told her to hurry back.

On her way to the bathroom, she noticed that their wedding garments were gone and replaced with two fluffy bathrobes on the door. Wow, she thought to herself, this hotel is first class! After splashing some water on her face and brushing her teeth, Kat pulled a tube of lipstick from her makeup bag. Carefully applying the deep ruby color to her lips, she leaned forward and kissed the glass, leaving a perfect image of her lips on the mirror. Blotting her lips with tissue, she stood back to view what she hoped JD would see when he made his way to the new bathroom. Deciding it needed something more, she took the lipstick out again and wrote a hastily crafted poem under the lip print:

Black as night horse
He rides the strong one
White as pure love
She is undone

As Kat returned to the bed wearing one of the bathrobes, she brought the other for JD and laid it on the end of the bed. He was wide awake now and made a comment about how wrong it was for someone to have provided her with cover, for he'd just have to remove it from her. "I'll save you the work, lazy bones." Kat said as she removed the bathrobe and let it drop to the floor. With that, JD flipped the covers back to invite her back into the bed with him.

As they snuggled against each other's bare skin, Kat heard a creak on the front step of the cabin. Startled, she pulled the covers up to her chin. Watching her reaction, JD whispered in her ear, "Did I tell you about the beach bears we have down here?" Kat looked over at him with wide eyes to see if he was serious. He just laughed out loud and informed her that he'd asked Bernardo to bring food from the kitchen when Carmen wasn't looking and drop it off for them.

"What?" Kat asked in her most shocked voice.

But JD stroked her bare arm and responded, "I didn't want a little thing like hunger to be an excuse for leaving this place!"

As Kat settled back into his arms, she traced JD's dark beard line with her finger before kissing him. This time there was not the urgency they had felt the night before. This time they knew they didn't have to leave the cabin for anything. This time their lovemaking was slow and steady. There was no doubt that Kat and JD were in love, and no doubt they would place each other first as they made their lives together.

CHAPTER 46

It wasn't until nearly 1:00 p.m. that Kat and JD emerged from their beach hideaway, and that was only to walk along the beach even further north. As they did, it dawned on Kat that she didn't know if he was to return to work tomorrow or what the normal pattern of their daily lives would be like. "Oh no, Kat, this is only the start of our honeymoon. Tomorrow I will take you to our capital city, La Paz, where we will continue having fun together. I want you to see more of Sur Baja, and frankly, I need to see more of you," said JD. "And, by the way," he continued, "that lipstick poem was great! Though I must also tell you that I love the poetry you write on my skin with your fingers each time you touch me."

Late in the day, the two had to concede that they were getting pretty hungry. After taking a shower together, they dressed for the trip back to the house. By now, most of the out-of-town guests had departed, either to catch flights or head back to La Paz. Walking slowly through the patio area where the tables and other items were stripped bare, JD opened the patio door and stuck his head in before letting Kat go in.

"Are you worried about something, JD?" Kat asked.

"Yes," he responded, "I'm worried that Carmen is going to throw something at me for not being here to say goodbye to the guests who left this morning!"

The two suddenly felt like intruders in their own home, but they made their way to the kitchen where they found Carmen stirring something on the stove. She didn't hear them enter, so JD went up to her and put his arms around her. She immediately turned around and began pointing her large wooden spoon at his chest while scolding him. He jumped back with his hands up in the air and then ran to stand behind Kat. Carmen couldn't help but break down and smile at his game. She told the two of them to go to the dining room, where she had provided an early dinner for his brothers, their wives, and the children so they could drive home on full stomachs.

When Kat and JD walked into the dining room, the children jumped off their chairs to run over to greet them. Even as their mothers protested, Gabino was tugging on JD's sleeve again. JD looked down to give Gabino his undivided attention when the little boy asked him a question in Spanish. Kat couldn't catch the whole question, but she could tell by JD's reaction that it must have been a doozy. JD shot an accusatory look at Pablo who was trying to appear very innocent as he pulled off another piece of bread from the loaf on the table. Kat asked JD what Gabino wanted, and JD put his hands on his hips and said, "Gabino tells me his father told him to ask me what you and I have been doing all this time. What shall I tell him?" Kat could feel the flush on her cheeks as she went speechless. JD then bent down to be near Gabino and said something that seemed to satisfy the little one who returned to his chair to eat. The adults were chuckling around the table, but Kat didn't know why.

JD leaned over to tell her that he told Gabino that they had been playing games and then got very sleepy. Kat realized she was going to have to get used to the antics of this new family... and resolved to throw herself into conversational Spanish as soon as they returned from La Paz.

By Monday morning, the household was cleared out, so Kat and JD brought their things from the cabin to the house to prepare for departure to La Paz for the week. Carmen had already changed the sheets and cleaned the master suite where the two would settle in.

They packed a single suitcase in order to head off across Baja to the beautiful city on the gulf. On the way, they stopped at the gravesite of JD's father to place there some wedding flowers that Carmen had been preserving.

The honeymoon days passed all too quickly, but the newlyweds made the nights last by the Sea of Cortez. Their love was easy. And their love was the start of a partnership that would yield plenty... on so many levels, in so many ways, and for so many people.

EPILOGUE

Juan Diego and Katarina Alvarez spent several more years in Todos Santos as JD built his business to numerous holdings. Eventually, he transferred most of the businesses in Mexico to César and turned the villa over to his younger brother who married a local girl. He and Kat moved to the United States, where they took up residence in San Diego and started a business together that combined their abilities. They became the first to design, manufacture, and sell beautifully colored concrete countertops for high-end homes. The very successful business allowed Kat to express her creativity, but she never stopped her private art pursuits. Selling under her maiden name, Steiner (which means stone in German), her sculptures are sought after by private collectors for homes and businesses.

On the side, JD maintained a stable for which he hired staff to board horses and run a riding school. He kept a direct hand in the work, and the school trained and sponsored several riders who went on to represent the United States in the Olympics. He was even instrumental in the creation of a foundation to further the competitive equestrian discipline and provide scholarships for children who would otherwise not have an opportunity to learn the sport.

Kat and Barb have remained best friends through the years. Mrs. Barb Cooper married just two years after Kat, and Barb and her husband reside in Riverside, California. They had a daughter on their own and later adopted a little boy who is profoundly deaf. Though Barb no longer works at the school for the deaf, she went on to publish a well-received textbook on total communication approaches in the education of special needs children.

Kat and JD returned to Todos Santos several times over the years. Each time they did, they stayed in the small cabin on the beach where they relived their honeymoon. Some of the more difficult visits, however, were the respective funerals of Carmen and Bernardo who passed away after decades of service to the Alvarez family.

After years of disappointment with not being able to conceive, Kat and JD eventually adopted twin infant boys from Mexico. Kat loved being a mother to her boys, and JD was a patient and fun-loving father. It wasn't long before both Carlos and Mateo were attending Kat's alma mater. Soon she and JD were the proud parents sitting in USC's Alumni Park watching them graduate.

As a graduation gift, they took the twins to Paris to visit the sights, including the newly remodeled Louvre. They even found the very sculpture that first drew them together. Later that same year, their sons met their respective wives who were best friends. That turn of events resulted in a double wedding the following year. They all concluded that there really must be something about being around Cupid that leads to love and marriage!

Now retired and living in the cottage in Carmel, Kat and JD have taken up golf, are active in their church, serve on various boards, and travel quite a bit. They particularly enjoy planning their annual trips to visit development projects in impoverished parts of the world where they sponsor many children and clean water projects through the charitable foundation they established for the purpose of making life better for children, families, and communities. They knew they had been blessed and were committed to being a blessing to others.

Through it all, their love held fast, and Kat still insists that JD is the sweetest kisser in the world.

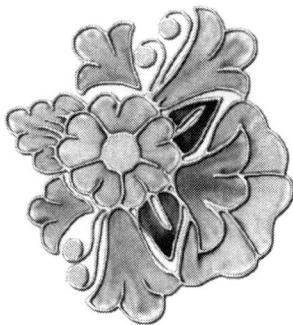

MORE FROM
RAYANNE SINCLAIR

If you enjoyed Beso Dulce, *be sure to read Rayanne Sinclair's first novel –* Steal Away!

When the smart and talented Anne Ledwell graduates from Penn State University in 1977, her parents gift her a trip to the British Isles. She's looking forward to the trip as a break from her frustrating job search in New York City, but the last thing she expects is to fall into the arms of a handsome Scottish balladeer.

Grant Donaldson is smitten with the young American woman after just one short evening together. He's committed to seeing her again, but how will she feel about him once she knows his past?

A powerful story about family, faith, friends, and strength of character, *Steal Away* will steal your heart.

Steal Away *is available in print and eBook versions at Amazon and Barnes & Noble online. For more information about her next book, please visit her website:*

http://rayannesinclair.com/

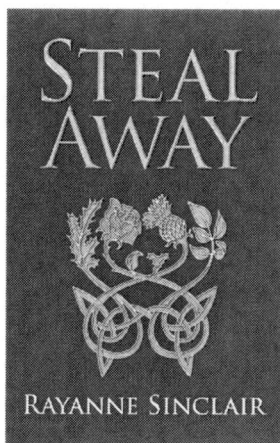

CPSIA information can be obtained
at www.ICGtesting.com
Printed in the USA
FFOW03n1727060614
5806FF